Monkey Men

Monkey Men

Bhima Prusty

Translated by
Jachindra Kumar Rout

BLACK EAGLE BOOKS
Dublin, USA

 BLACK EAGLE BOOKS

USA address:
7464 Wisdom Lane
Dublin, OH 43016

India address:
E/312, Trident Galaxy, Kalinga Nagar,
Bhubaneswar-751003, Odisha, India

E-mail: info@blackeaglebooks.org
Website: www.blackeaglebooks.org

First International Edition Published by
BLACK EAGLE BOOKS, 2023

MONKEY MEN
by **Bhima Prusty**
Translated by **Jachindra Kumar Rout**
Cell: 7008758624

Original Copyright © **Bhima Prusty**
Translation Copyright © **Jachindra Kumar Rout**

Cover & Interior Design: Ezy's Publication

ISBN- 978-1-64560-481-5 (Paperback)
Library of Congress Control Number: 2023950822

Printed in United States of America

FROM TRANSLATOR'S PEN...

Truth has to be known by experiences. No belief can help you on the way; all beliefs are barriers. I talk about this experiences that I have come upon at the time of converting the thoughts of one language to other language. A reader may discover himself amidst the tribal, when he set out the journey into the tribal stories in this text. I am sure around 360° that nothing excepts the truth is described in the stories. The writer has moved from forest to forest, one tribe to other tribes to gain the experiences about the practical situations that happen to tribal people; problems, the face, the exploitation in which they are victimised, help of the government, setting of Industries, displacement, rehabilitation, sufferings, all the practical situations have enriched the themes of the stories full-fledged.

Not possible, I do admit that, the tribal stories in Odia language by using exact tribal termilogy has ever written, the loudable attempt what Bhima Prusty started in Odia literature. I have tried the best to preserve all the original feelings of the writer in translated language. The termilogy of tribal people what the writer has used did not find appropriate words in English language. That is the exact problem that the translation meets at the time of translation.

Jachindra Kumar Rout

FROM AUTHOR'S PEN

The tribal lives are to be die out. What appears, after someday, this tribe will remain as a word in future. One day, this vast and the ancient tribal inhabitant will efface.

Most of us have not seen this inhabitant this is about to efface, they are only heard like a story by the people of city dwellers. They are assessed by very few people those who have come upon them in person. It is very rare people don't know the reason why they prefer to reside in dense forest amidst the rill, hills. Some outsiders, they prefer to stay with them in spite of unfavourable condition for different intentions. Particularly, the stay there temporarily for preparing the film, documentary and research etc. Many things have been prepared on them.

I, myself involved with the tribals of Koraput, Kalahandi, Kandhamal district of Odisha since two decades. A kind of intimacy has spontaneously been developed among them during my stay with them along with the social activists and organisers in their tribes. I have extended my co-operation and dedicated times for the awareness of the tribes against the multinational companies and made them conscious to fight for their land water forest and hills. I have travelled from forest to forest, village to village on feet to carry out the work success. People those who have lost their lives in that fighting, some pillars were constructed in their memory. When the tribals could not able to continue the spirit or fighting, at last they surrender their lands to the company and displaced with compensation from the land of their ancestors and move to other states for their livelihood.

Due to owners outrage, many of them are migrating to neighbour states as daily wagers. There, they are exploited and forced to do excess labour and died of malnutrition, diseased and without food. On the otherhand, some religious fundamentalists have kept themselves busy in converting them into their religion. The regular and continuous conflict in between the tribal and non tribals have compelled them to leave the place for ever, as a result of which these people are bound to live in town and city as daily wagers by leaving their permanent residence.

It is seen, some organisers take initiative for the Boarding, lodging, education of tribal children with the funding of foreigners. In later period, the same tribal children being educated in modern city style forget all about their own culture and tradition.

There is no end of suffering and exploitation of the tribal people because the landlords and zamindars were exploiting them in pre independent era and now the politicians and the wine dealers are doing the same job as before. It is only time has been changed, but there is no compromising in suffering and exploitation.

These tribe lover tribals have been suffering and affected due to mismanagement of administration and they search for a rejected place to build their huts to earn their livelihood in town and city. The same sorts of fear, instability and no alternative are seen among tribals like the people of city. The long preserved forest, hill and lands of the tribals have lost their identity and existence. There is continuous process of digging of mines and deforestation is going on uninterrupted. The social activists have made the tribals pur in the chess board of income.

Many innocent tribals are sacrificed in the fighting of police and maoists. For all these reasons, the tribals are floating in the favour of displacement. The practical and real experiences that I have gained during my stay with them to realise their struggle against modern civilisation and exploitation which have inspired me to preserve these burning situations in my writings, particularly, their culture, tradition and live style and struggle and displacement are the main sources and elements for the theme of my writings will remain as the records for these tribal people.

I know their lives have been written in many languages. But the writings about tribals lives, do not bear the colloquial language of the tribal people except writing their lives, for which I may consider them as incomplete tribal literature. Even the writers have not gone into that interior area where the communication facility is impossible, what I have made possible.

I understand, unless the writer's entity entered into that part of their lives practically, the reality can't come out for the revealment of the real situation. What I know, you may smell the reality, instead of them, in my writings. They were there existed, these stories stands as the evident of it.

Prof. Dr. Bhima Prusty
Original Writer of the stories

CONTENTS

COLD BLOOD

Wonderful! A lot of people have made a crowd on the block campus. All were loitering on veranda, road, everywhere. Someone was shouting from crowds, Maikanch, Maikanch, wherever they gathered. B.D.O. sir had not reached till that time. The morning sun was growing old waiting for the arrival of BDO sir.

One room, roofed by asbestos was sealed out of many rooms. A woman was feeding breast to her baby sitting on that lonely yard. That two hankers stumbled upon the scene of a half naked woman feeding her child sitting isolatedly. A shrewed man asked tactfully, "Are the one out of that gathering people those who have come to this place?"

The woman stood out of shame and drop marshaled her sari viewing the male persons before her. She had worn a green blouse matching with a striped saree and made a bagpacked with a napkin in which she put the baby inside that.

"Who are you? What happened with you?" They asked. She had closed the door of tears and sealed her mouth since long. Her lips were opened spontaneously to vomit all her over loaded agony before that two government employees and told, "I am Suvarna Jhodia, wife of martyr Abhilas Jhodia.

The squint clerk was standing there. He laughed at her statement, "What do you mean? Had he become martyr at the bullet of British government?" he had acted upon the word 'salvation' in such a manner that Suvarna got angry instantly. My marada (male) has lost his life by bullet by the instruction of BDO. The company had motivated them to shoot us. The man died of fighting for our forest, lands, water is certainly martyr for us.

Two clerks couldn't look at the glaring of Suvarna. They realised that widow Jhodiari must have been motivated by the outside literate persons. She speaks their language. She became wild and violent at the death of her husband. You don't have any work with us, you may talk about the martyr before the BDO after he returned from Kamani tour.

"The BDO will give back to my male, marada." That middle aged persons had left the place before listening anything.

The baby slept peacefully in Napkin bag after breast feeding. The sheet of catnap had covered her eyes – she dreamed that she was reaping the ripe crops in the fields. The waves of Suran, Kandula, Make maze mandia were playing in wind in the patch of one acre of land. She felt some one reaping crops like a shadow. He might be her male. His sense came back. She felt her baby crying she came rushing to give mandia podding to her baby. Her father is watching his child drinking jurum-wine. Accurately resembled to his father. He vanished when she reached there. Again he had to come back to the place of reaping. Again he appeared at the place of work. When she turned up and found him disappeared. She can't focus on reaping the crops. She is climbing up the danger, hill. The ripen crops of her male's cultivation was smiling from that shifted cultivation. "I can't reap many crops all alone myself." She cried loudly on the Danger hill hopelessly. Her male Duma, the ghost is cleansing tears from her cheek.

The calendar of 16th December 2000 and the glistening of the sun shine on her tear wet eyes was hanging before her. Number of police vans are running towards the village from that calendar. Judhistira Jhudia of the village snappished all the Andira, Marda, male in to forest-Danger. She could see the backside, how her male was climbing up the Danger. Two big vehicles and six jeeps reached at Maikanja. The hundred of police got down from vehicles, shoes, guns and entered into her villages. Dhanei Jhodiari, the elder mother, Badama of Judhistira Jhodia had left all the females, Dhangdies, maiji those who were inside the rooms, all stood before the police out of fear. The circle inspector of Raigada entered into village, shouting loudly and being followed by Gurkha armed police. Golak Badjena, the BDO of Kasipur was sitting silently inside the jeep at Maikanj Chowk. Suvas Swain, shouting with threatening, "O nonsense Judhistira Jhodia, Prakash Jhodia, Prabhudan Nayak and the Suvash Nayak, you all nonsense come up. Let me see who will save you today? You all have stopped the works of the company, you are saying, all the water, jungle, lands, jala, jami, jangle yours. Are these danger lands of your inheritance? You became leaders at the risk of rules and regulations. Do you think me Kasipuria police? I have come from Cuttack, absolutely Katikia. I declared five minutes time for you, if you fail, then I will let you know who am I? Listen! The BDO sir has come with us with Magistrate power. No one will save you today! You brother in laws, sale." Holding with her baby and other twos beside her she was standing in the company of the Maiji, the women. No word in her mouth. One of the maijies dared to ask, "Why do you search for them?" It's only four minutes more, where have you kept them hidden infrom us, otherwise get yourself ready to receive beating." Whosoever you may be, no matter if you are the tribal women. Suvash Swain is to listen nothing. He was looking like a male cat. Dhanei Jhodiani was trying to make Suvash Swain understand that there was no male person home today. You may tell us if you really want to tell anything. We will inform them, if there is any message for them.

Three minutes more, tell us where the male persons of Maikanch hiding? I will beat you hard. Suvash Swain's ear was pluged and mouth was blaring. The Gurkha police was delving for them in huts one after another. The women of Maikanj were averting them by interlocking their hands. There was scuffle in between the police and the Maijis of Maikanja. Krushna Mohapatra, the photographer was taking shapes of the screen standing among them. He tells, "Nonsense, Maikanja's people! You were obstructing us last day. Where will you go today? Where will you hide yourself? You nonsense tribal woman come up front. How will you hide your males today? Let me see?" Police were hitching to Dhanei jhodiari was arguing waving hands. The old woman of fifty three years old fell thrashing. Another photographer Sangrami Dandasena was prompting to police, "beat them to that nonsense hard." The male Andira will come up from their hidden places at the beating to women, maiji."

Suvash Swain threatening, "Beat that maijis." Police applied lathi charged. She put her three children under her belly and bent over them from police attack. Police beating Dhanei Jhodia rolling down the street. The legs and backside of all maiji wealed and lamented rolling on the ground. They all cry for Dhanei Ma, "Hey! Police will kill our Dhanei Ma."

This bawling sound echoed by the nearby Danger where the male-maradas were hiding. "Dhanei ma died."

This whispering spread over among all the males. They all came down the Dangara confused. Police stood pointing their guns towards Dangar, hill. There was another senior flatter, Phatkar Bhaskar Rao, he was encouraging police in loud voice, "Finish them in firing. I will take care whatever consequence comes. Will they live to protect the company?"

Suvas Swain was shouting, "Fire-Fire-shoot them dead."

Cracking sounds of gun powder and fire was resounding the Dangar. Some of the maiji rushing in front of the gun, "kill us… kill us we are ready. Don't kill our males. Everywhere there was smoke and fire. The shot of the gun striked at the leg of Ganga of Kucheipada village. He was writhing rolling on the ground. Dhanei, who lost her consciousness, she looked scoull. Another shoot of the gun striked at the leg of a cowherd, Arjun Jani, eleven years old child. The hidden people those who were coming down the Dangar, at the death news of Dhanei ma. They climbed up the Dangar again at the ceaseless firing of the police. Forest has lost herself in the smoke of Gun powder. Suvash Swain is convincing to BDO sir, leave it sir, people died at cease fire, let them others go; the rest will certainly be in your clutch. All the flatters, Phatkara are laughing at the sayings of Suvash Swain. Police are approaching towards jeep. Mr. BDO has been sitting bent down his head. Silently inside the jeep from beginning to end. Purna Jhodia and Ghasi Jhodia were falling on the road and writhing out of pain, police have taken them in jeep. The police have set fire to their rannsaked jeep to justify their actions against tribal people. The jeep on fire was being put out by Sita Jhodia and other maiji after the police left the place.

Males are coming back home from Dangar one after other. She is delving her own marada, male among them.

Suvas Jhodia, Arjun, Maheswara Majhi all were shouldering Parasu Jhodia from Dangar. They all were striked by Gun. People those were not injured by guns, they came back home. But where was her Marada? They have made sleep in open field three dead bodies. She ran to that place madly.

She is trying to recongnise the dead body one after other. No! This is not. This is Damodar Jhodia of Baghri Jhola. The bullet has passed through from back to front. Dead body searches the dead body. No this is Raghunath Jhodia, bullet had entered in arm pit and ousted in backside. And who is this one? bullets ousted through his eyes. She fell thrashing on the dead body. Everything appeared to her gloomy. Many things heard to her whimping. He was cultivating – doing Kamani which company will understand how the family of the person is maintained, who was earning in daily wages, Kamani? Will she burnish utensil in the house of company for feeding her three children? Again she will have to nourish them. She will keep herself engaged in daily wages. The scene of Mulabali Nayak of Srungar village appears before her, out of these incidents. She faced a lot of problems to managing her family. She did work in the house of Ishrafil, the man who came for survey of Aluminium company got her married and became his maiji.

The scene of Dhangdi's daughter Sunari Nayak of Sagabali village who was working in the residence of Nibedan Patra and later became his Maiji permanently.

The face of Kuni Majhi appears before her. She became concubine of the man Thakur Das, who came from Kolkata. She turned up Maiji of him. Thakur Das has escaped separately. But she is carrying the children of Thakur Das and begging alms from door to door. She suffers a lot alike distiller.

What will happen to her life next? She speaks her dreams loudly to herself in soliloque – No – No, her sleep had broken after that. Suvarna Jhodiani got up by squeezing up her eyes. The afternoon sun shine had disappeared from Block's yard. The thought of heartless scene of that day, as if took away the sense of eyes, ears, mouth from her for some moments. She became relaxed by and by she found that baby had got up from sleep and was playing with himself inside the napkin bag.

Her own people were loitering on the yard's of veranda. BDO sir was expected to come. All had waited for him but he was delaying. They will place a demand letter before him. They will let him listen their complaint. The bald headed be spectacled Head clerk came flying like a raven to them. He told, "BDO sir has gone on tour, Kaman. If you want give that application to BDO Sir, you may give that to me. I am the head clerk of this office. I will handover that letter to BDO sir."

Whatever it may be, whosoever you may be, we won't give this application to no one but BDO sir. People did not obey him. The head clerk wanted to know about the content of that demand application.

We have been in ferment for jungle, water, lands since eight years. The agent and brokers of company are motivating police to bit and kill us. If we lodge a complaint in police station. They never respond us no more. The demand of the people reached on peak by and by. Someone had told, "We will demand before BDO sir, You're sitting at Maikanch from beginning to end. You're witness of the situation how the police shoot down three people dead in your presence. They became martyr.

Let me ask him, How many times you'll let the company kill our tribal people through police.

I will ask him, one had been complaining by gripping the bleeding anger before the Government. At the same time the vehicle of BDO Sir had reached. The head clerk escaped to his seat. The BDO got down and had entered into his office directly bending his head. All people were shouting stopped at once. Someone let another man show. "This is Golak Badjena." Oh! This one?

Suvarna saw that man. Oh! This man. This man had ordered the police to fire, sitting inside the vehicle.

BDO had allowed ten to twelve people into his office. He received the letter of demand from them and listened their complaint/ allegation. Suvarna entered into office by joggling some people. Her eyes were glaring by fire light. The baby of one month was playing inside the napkin bag. The peon whispered at the year of BDO. This one sir. Suvarna Jhodia, wife of Abhilash Jhodia.

Golakh Badajena, the BDO, sat bending his head just like the day of firing inside the vehicle. Suvarna had thought of speaking many things to BDO sir, but the gust of anger and discontent chocked at the throat and returned to her belly wine pressed her chest. She heard how the bullets had passed though her husband's eyes in the speed of lighting. She vomited poisons–

"O BDO Sir, Ajna

Give me food

Keep me, keep my children.

The weight of her words were more weightful than bullets. BDO became imbalanced and nodded his head. The widow woman, Jhodiani and a baby in the napkin cradle was hanging by neck, his eyes were glimmering; he was child of Abhilash Jhodia. When the eyes of the BDO and eyes of the child united, the head of the BDO became low down than before.

Just after eight months of these incident, the BDO died of certain unknown disease. Suvarna had made herself understand that the curse and tears of her children burn the BDO in disease alive. But will her male come back again?

Once Prafulla Pradhan, the Sub-Collector of Raigada had reached at Maikanga being escorted by his body guards and peon. All the people of the village stood around the sub-Collector at Benanmunda, the meeting place of the village. He declared one lakh rupees compensation along with ten thousand rupees by National Family scheme for the widow of Abhinash Jhodia which will be given away to the heir.

Judheswar Jhodia, got angry and told, "We will kill Suvash Swain and give two lakh rupees to his widow wife. Are you agree?"

What happened at Maikanj. That day, the law will punish the criminal. Now Suvarna Jhodia needs to receive the compensation for the maintenance of her family. This rupee will undoubtedly grow the family economically.

No, we don't need any compensation, will Abhinash Jhodia come back with your money? No, we don't need your money. People were obdurate in their insistence. At last sub-Collector told 'Ok' let me know the intention of the heir. Let her speak.

Suvarna stood in front of the government. When ever she stands before the government people one picture flash before her eyes i.e., the terrific scene and sound of the bullet passing through the eyes in the speed of lightening. I will be satisfied the day when you will split the blood of the killer on the Duma of my male, Suvarna told tumbling and tandeming.

The Sub-Collector left the place in his vehicle. People raised their voices strong for jungle, jami and jala. The people of Maikanja built three temple of mantry beneath the Danger after names of Abhinash Jhodia, Damodar and Raghunath Jhodia and engraved their names on plates.

The unending thought of Managing of family without a male had over clouded her mind. Everything was there. She was there, but she was quite closed like shadow after the Kamani of her male. Presently the burden of cultivation work increased a lot. Tilling the land, spading, weeding, sowing seeds, let them ripe then milling them to rice and boiling for rice. The work is completed. The same thing is applied for kandul dal. Peeling the Kusuma and cook them then oil will come up after it grinded. all process in agriculture is need to reach the final stage.

After a long processing the thing come last. She was busy to find time to take rest. In the busy schedule dissuading birds from field, selling crops in bazaar, buying grocery, biscuits, managing home with that money is not a small matter.

As per the tradition of Jhodia family, the sons or daughter will have to be separated from parents to take care of his own family after marriage. They will have to manage with the production of the patches of land that he has got on separation. After death of Abhilash the responsibility of death was prevail upon her. They found Suvarna as factor of the death of their son, Abhilash. They were not involved in any affairs. Her brother-in-law, brother of Abhinash was quite discontent with her regarding that property affairs. She was quite alone without any others support. Her children were growing like the height of Salap tree.

Sometimes she cries looking at the martry temple of her male when she passed that way. Now a days the Duma of Abhilash is not visible. Suvarna among four family members was doing her works voiceless in the world of poverty. People of the village and nearby villages gather there to observe the martry's day on every 16th December. Reputed speanery were invited to that function to deliver speech in the occasion. They emphasis on the right of the tribals on lands, forests and water. There is a grand celebration of dance, song, music. All were reciting "Abhilash Jhodia be immortal". But the stream of tears were not stopped from her eyes. There was martyr's day every year. There was no crowd of Kandha, Jhodia's, no crowd and no warmness in speech of the speaker. There was no whispering, no hot in temperature and no one was dying for tribals. There was no ferment, movement, general meeting, vehicles stop programme now a days. Those who were in front line of agitation, they were trapped by Fatkara and Malkaria. All the Kandha, Jhodia, Harijana. They were organising people not for lands but for compensation money.

Suvarna came to know, the mother of the martyr Raghunath Jhodia of Baghrijholi was receiving interest from the compensation money is giving her figure prints every month. She has got the news of wife of Damodar Jhodia who had already received the compensation money i.e., one lakh ten thousand. The news of about the people of Barigan, Borigma, Sialapadara, Baghamari, Paidaguda and Sinjam who had received the compensation money from Government. People were shouting for compensation money. The organisations, social activists have decamped from Kasipur one after another. The voice of the people for forest land and water was disappeared in forest and Danger by and by. Suvarna was regularly listening these news of tribal people detent nations. But she failed to weed out pari grass from her crop field. All her three children were wandering here and there in the woods. One and half of her lands was left uncultivated. Teachers were not regular to the schools.

It was quite difficult on her part to manage her children out of that productions from field. Her waist was bending down by poverty and troubles of the children. Right this time her brother in law, Trinath reached her home along with certain important papers and ink accompanied by Government officers. He tried to convinced, how long will you live in starvation without giving the patches of lands to father and son? Do you think about these three children? Government people say to educate these children leaving them in boarding of Ashram school. The interest for eight thousand rupees will come to your account every month. So you could live well."

Suvarna understand. Her brother-in-law has been separated from parents after marriage to the daughter of Judhistira Jhodia and live happily. He was quarrelling for lands when he was unmarried. Now he has come to her like Phatkata gentle man and wants to educate his nephews. Trinath went on speaking we belong to same family, think deeply we three families lives separately.

Her nose ring, Jambli, hanging from nose to mouth shook hearing the matter of family. The family relationship had put her in the thoughts of to be and not to be. Having heard about this from brother-in-law she swayed her body like a drunkard and entered into the dark kitchen. There, the smoke was rising in circle from the half-burnt fuel wood from the hearth. All the earthen pots were darkened by that smoke. There were Aluminium utensils, half-burnt fragmentary sal leaf's pinka kept on Niche by her Male marada, Nautumba, Goud Pots of different sizes were falling of Abhilash her male would come to speak her about right decision, this thought stricked her mind. Eyes burn smoke, filled her eyes tears, "Tell me what should I do? Should I stay alone or away from family?"

As if the Duma was standing before to listen to her. Tomorrow, all these woods, lands and water will not be with us. How these three children will get live? Where will they stay? Rather let them educate and settle in job elsewhere.

There was no answer of so many questions. Is it the Duma at Abhilash had been disappeared in the narrow flow of Kajakada river, sal forests, in the climbers of Kurei flower? She could see about many unknown diseases and the days of starvation in the darkness. She came out of the cave of dark-kitchen – Duma never takes any decision, but human being Trinath, the brother-in-law handed over all papers to her hand and pressed her left thumb print on that ink pad. Suvarna shivered out of cool. All the thought and ability of protection preserved in her all flew away from her and vanished.

DEAR MR.

Trees goes fast with multiple greenery, if they are manured by human blood. Who is that Duma, God may know, who had put such type of superstitious things in the mind of Tribals. Tadapenu, the God of Earth had bathed in the hot blood of Dhangdas, the youngsters. The more patches of Turmeric lands one has, the more reputation of the name and fame of him. 'Head's' sacrifices are needed for more production. Many male buffalos and sacrifices are regular practice.

Both natives and British, the invaders enjoyed different laws. Sacrifices were eradicated after a long blood shedding and violence protestation. Blood shedding replace the blood bathing Meria, male Buffalo. After one hundred and fifty years, the customers are in quest of that blood bathing turmeric. Customers want to taste that old turmeric. Demands for Kandhamala's turmeric rose in lips and bound in large decree. The business became hot by the names of Kandhamala's turmeric.

He hid beneath the breast of the forest and hills accompanied by his children. All his children and wife were sleeping on the spread skirt of her saree. Sleep was in dream. The patches of well grown turmeric filed of two acres lands was waving in his dream. A ray of vindication spread in him.

Right now, the turmeric will be supplied, that will be the product of fresh blood, flesh bone, sweats of people. Curry of this quality added turmeric will be more tasty and delicious. The colour of that turmeric will be more deep, rather red orchre.

The red orchre's thoughts shifted his eyes to the ships, stalls of road side chouk, and flags and flags fluttering in front of some selected houses all that he had left behind. Everywhere, he found fluttering of orchre colour flags beside the highway side's temples of Lord Hanuman of Vajrang Party. On the top cross symbols of fragmentary dilapidated church.

There is a national flag, perhaps all have forgotten about this. One party had removed the Ashok's symbol from middle portion and placed the symbol of his own party. The flags of different colours were trying to frighten me if they get any chance.

He is not that fool, he could not understand the matter of cold-war in between red and saffron colour flags of two parties. People having lost their lands and houses in the conspiracy of all that flags, hid in the forest and observing the activities of the people beneath the mountain. Smoke of burning village was rising up into the sky. But they were still in anxiety, in fear of least they cold search forest up them. The wounded eyes were not in rest of watching if they approach.

They must be tried of burning the villages one after another. It is sure, they must have carried all the ransacked things from all villages, their villages must be 10 to 15 kms remote from this plots. They must be prescheduled to ransack other villages. We may not be in their mind in such horrible situation and hurried mood.

Inability led them to think the words of consolidation to themselves, wherever, there was any blank space in the forest, minimum three to four family people gather there in limited area, with great adjustment. They had forgotten and kept aside everything. The faces of all persons look alike. Their faces were resembling to the dark face of night and they were swarming like wild black ants in one place.

There was no food in the stomach. All people, starting from child to old all have been waiting since twenty-four hours for one night and one day. Rice pot had cracked on fire-hearth. The thoughts of children as if removed from their mind. Moving from one place to another place out of hunger to locate a brook in the forest. They stopped the mouth of children by pressing their mouths with cloth. This search and business had made them forget about children's precarious condition. Any sorts of sound may put them in problem and create a new fearsome scene for them. They were very much conscious of the rest of their lives.

Often in wonder, he gazed at the faces of his family members whom he had brought into forest saving their lives. They all laying liveless out of tiredness or walking long distance into forest. Both his diseased son and daughter were resting their heads in the lap of his wife, she had wrapped them in skirt. It is only face of the daughter in which mosquitoes were swamming over. She swayed the mosquitoes and wrapped her face with another saree. He could never think that such type of situation would come over him, he would wonder in forest like a Gypsy he had never dreamt this in life.

He could sense, there must be certain danger approaching very closely. He has a news, that a secret meeting was commenced in the neighbouring village, Tiangia. Joseph Digal, of his neighbour had already received a bearing letter by his name. It is told, "Joseph, if you want to live a live with your family members, you give up the work of postering; Abandon your propanda and let this information reach to Hindu Samaj, live a life; no time to chat a lot – Jai Hind."

They, in the same night did have the performance of firework at Tiangia village. The forest, was echoed of their ado. They all were excited in anger after rulling the villagers of Tiangia, they became blood thirsty and over ran in hundreds of number from three sides of their village. The businessmen of the coastal villages of Odisha those who had opened their stalls were in front line and others women, girls, old woman, Dhangda, Dhangdi, Maiji were accompanied by them. All were carrying a weapon's each in their hands, such as Harpoor, cub, hoe, Hammer, Kerosin and petrol fuel.

There were two prayer hall in Lingagada villages, one was of Baptist and other one was of Catholics. Some people had climbed to the asbestos roof of a prayer hall and begun to strike with Hammer. They entered into the hall and piled all the papers, photographs of Jesus Christ, Bible and many furniture, in one place, poured petrol on it and set fire. Two to three people climbed to the pillar that was holding the cross symbol. They beat the cross symbol with hammer and turned it up trident.
All had made up their mind to leave the village for forest. They ran away with their bag and bandages and babies. But he was not ready to leave home, for which, he rather had bolted the gate inside.

Gobardhan, an unreputed political worker of his village, was locating the house of the people to the officers who had set fire. He was almost deciding where to hoist the saffron colour flags and which one will be set fire. He having himself inside the room, was developing a positive thought about him, that they would not do any harm to him as he was the only lawyer of the panchayat. He calls him babu babua, what was the nick name, being called like this by him. All the problems he had in Tahasil about the records of lands, Gobardhan babu solved all that. He was doing all works with taking any fees. He attends all the festive occasion of all the villagers with interest without any hesitation. They come to attend the Christmas day, cut cake on Christmas day. They all eat delicious fruits here. He, to all villagers, had made their names like uncle, aunt, sister-in-law and many. He, what he remembers had never done any harm to anyone in his life. He was carrying his business in Tahasil as well as works in cultivation lands to manage his family. He not only in the village, rather, all over the panchayat was widely popular having the name and fame with much regards to himself.

Yes! The only crime, what other community feels, that he was a Christian. How could he be responsible for his baptisation, because before hundred years, his forefathers were converted to Christianity, he was not new to he what he is now that is on the basis of hereditary. With no one, but with himself, he had continued the legal argument and with his family members too. Three generations had already passed accepting Christianity. Still, these questions remain very fresh within him why, the tribal people of this generation are converting themselves to Christianity. These questions are also active in him why we accepted Christianity? Or why we became Hindu? After all we are Adivasi, we are neither Christian nor Hindu. It was unknown how could people divide our tribals into two groups and what was the attraction? I don't understand this? Who motivated Adivasis against Adivasis in blood battle? Nothing strikes to his mind.

When the fire of giddiness smoulder in mind, people in that state of mind they kick other's request and appeal. The same thing happened. They heard the sound of striking of Hammer to break the Iron Gate, root of the houses.

He could hear the breaking sound of his rib. They broke the doors and entered into the rooms. They found him standing with the grown-up, college going daughter and diseased son, who held the hands of their father and stood in both sides. But his wife had caught hold him from backside. In the meantime, four young men dragged him outside of the room from their clutch. They devasted his village before his eyes. Some of them had climbed on the asbestos roof like monkey and were beating them into pieces. Some of them were digging grills from the building. They had set fire with the huts of the village. The village was on fire. Some people were carrying the furniture, utensils and home appliances very quickly. Some plunderers cut the heads of the goats for feast.

People, in front of his residence had been waiting for him. No one of his village except him was present there. Someone had given a fist at back of his neck and asked, "Do you want life or death?"

"Will you agree. What we demand?"

"Yes! Yes! I will do."

"Then you beg pardon to Gobardhan Babu, bend your head fall flat on his feet."

He looked to front. Gobardhan Pradhan was standing in the company of miscreant. All the stupids : his wife Mula Pradhan, Nirakar Sahoo, Bibhuti Pradhan, Viswanath Malik, Suna Malik, Babina Pradhan, Dusashan Nayak and many were present there, all known persons were there. Perhaps ten to twelve people of his village, who had saffron colour flags on their roofs and they were save. That is why they joined their hands with outsiders and observed the drama of devastation silently. Once he was fighting for them in the court but no one was there to protect him. He had no alternative but fell on the feet of Gobardhan Pradhan saying, "Pradon me, Babu Babua."

"Who will save to whom, if you want to join your hand with us and let us move to set fire in the houses of others", asked Gbbardhan Pradhan.

He held tight the feet of Gobardhan Pradhan and begged pardon, "Babu Babu you know that I am a lawyer, I am working for law, how could I take law onto me?"

Mula, Gobardhan's wife from the crowd made a face and told, "Why you have hidden your wife? Call her, let her join her hands with us."

He moved the feet of Mularani, "Babuani O' Esteemed Queen, you know my wife, she is a UP School teacher. How could a teacher do this? Could she break the house of anyone? Would she able to set fire in the houses of her students?"

Someone from the crowd shouted unseen, "Then let your daughter come with us." He told regretfully, "My daughter is studying under graduate in a college, is it possible on the part of an educated girl like her?"

A sound floated in air, "then let your son come with us."

"My son a diseased one, he scare of water and fire. He fears of high sound and noise. How could an underage boy do such type of miscreation?"

"You, nonsense became very shrewd. Your education has made you clever. Being a lawyer you talk such type irrelevant things."

He peeped to see the man giving such remark, He was one of his uneducated friends who always had presumptions remark on his education and law business.

He had envious of his well to do status. As if this was the chance for him to put down and abase.

He felt that, all these affronts was not for his Christianity, rather they were a chance to repay their wrath of jealously. Though he could understand the intention of the mob, still he had not given up felling on the feet of every and each irritants continuously. It was acquisition of personal vindication. Now he stood up right. All on sudden, someone had kicked at his backside.

"We have nothing to tell. Only demand we have, you convert to Hindu with all your members, otherwise we will set fire in your family."

"One of the coastal belt residence let him listen the final decision."

'Yes! I will become Hindu.'

'Then drink the water of cow dung.'

'His nose irritated, still he agreed.'

Yes , I will drink cowdung-water.'

A laugh out bursted. Someone ordered to bring. A man came with a mug full of cow dung – water in the jug.

He drank all that in a quaff.

He was blindly running after all that superstitious condition only to save his life. In spite all that agreement; they didn't have trust on him. They all striked with hammer on his trustfulness. Now you go and bring the Bible from home and put that on fire.

He became speechless for a moment. If you were told to put the Gita on fire, would you do that? The fire of rebel burning in him, but he tripped his heel and controlled the wrath – Yes! There are many like me. If they were in my position they would throw the Gita into fine. Why should he not do that? There was a consine Bible in question. He entered into the room to bring that book. Before this, a young man had packed all his books, utensils in polly pack, pen stand, table cloth, brass flower base and searching for money everywhere. All his law books were fallen scattered. The pillow and bed pillow were turned upside. That boy was trying to break the Godrej Almirah.

He stopped for a moment, all that items of home appliances and money etc. but in the presence of the owner, that created problem and trouble him. All had lift home for forest. Why this man left behind. That young man grumbled his presence. He instructed him, leave this place immediately. If you want to save your life, they are here in the planned programme to convert you to Hindu. They know, by heart you can't be Hindu. They just want to put down you, abase you and beat you and they may rape your daughter and wife before you and throw your son into fire.

He had come to take Bible, as they demanded to surrender that before them, but the plunderer exposed all about their plans which paniced him. He trembled out of fear. He scrabbled from room to room and searched his wife and children. The back door was opened completely. He went to backside thatched house and groped in cowshed. They were under the belly of cow. He detethered the cow and calf. He picked up his son on the chest, caught hold the daughter's hand and called his wife impressively – not to stay here. Let us move.

He went rushing through the Turmeric land, rear word of the house into forest – All members of family were running keep abreast of him out of panic. The morning was opening his eyes. The long journey for a long distance to reach Ningaged through the forest hill of Ningagad, Gadiakal village, Jakana Forest, daughter fell unconscious. The day became night his daughter had lost her sense at the trial of bringing back the sense of daughter by flushing water on her face, that took sometimes. There at Nilungia all the thatched houses were turned up ashes. The houses were left, there was not a single man inside. He couldn't feel, how could he reach in Nilungia forest again.

That horrible dark night was closing her eyes. People, hidden in Nilungia forest were in search of a bourn for morning work. All were coming down of the forest hill towards plane lands at the growth of day. He, along with his family members, was in the race of that people.

Reaching at G-Udaygiri hill, they found their number was very few. People in hundred no, hidden in the forest-hills with them, all reached at the street. The bag and baggages of tin box, attachi, utensils, the cage of pet parrots were with them. They all had crowded the city like the wondered Bedwin.

Due to tiredness, his family members, were became so feeble that they could not keep abreast of the crowd out of fatigue. His daughter had trodden upon a poisonous thrown, indeed that was surged to out but she could not walk smoothly but hobbled. They, first drank water up to brim and he let them hold a biscuit pocket each.

The camp, in which the police officers, Tahasildar, BDO, CRPF Police, soldiers all were busy and seemed active in their activities. He registered his name and entered into joggled into crowd to get a polythene for a tent. He entered into the world of fantacy.

The carpet was spread inside the rug that was given away to him. There were five families, consist of not less than thirty members including baby, infant and children had to adjust themselves in that over crowd place. However, he held over bit by bit and could succeed and settled with a little space for sitting and sleeping for his family members.

The relief camp was more safer than his village and forest. The divastaters, as well as rebellions didn't have any fear either of police or of administrators. They had made all of them their puppets in their hands. But, they had fear of soldiers who were watching the camp outside. Otherwise, they were very careless for others.

The camp was surrounded by the throne fence. The motor bikes were stopped outside of the fence. They were sadistically deriving pleasure how the homeless people of thirty villages were passing their times like insects. They were passing comments and laughing at us.

The CRPF soldiers were dissuading them from that place by saying Go away, go away. But the rebellions did also let the homeless people listen their warning with browbeat.

"How long these military men watch you, let us see? Outside the camp, politics got privilege to keep the atmosphere warm. The oppressor's crocodile tears was creating a scene for the oppressions. There was peaceful procession going on. For these oppressions the social activists and specialist were coming to the camp to see the precarious condition of human-cattle of the tent. One after another, they were consulting with people. There was a flow of reporters, both electronic and print media to the camp. There was continuous flow of vehicles of the political leader and ministers to the camp.

We have killed the sage, there is no link with the matter of Christians – Moos', were distributing their posters underground.

They did have disregards to them. These were the international conspiration against the Hindu culture for its complete ruine – activities of the Christian goons.

There were no stop of fire to the houses behead the

head of CRPF soldiers. Some were engaged in making hue and cry.

He came out of the tent for certain work and assured his wife to come back within an hour. He was in doubt after giving signature on the gate pass register. If he goes there CRPF will write. Mr such and such.

The names of the parties will be there. He will have to write detailed about his arson and stealing of appliances and will request them for drastic action against accused – what will be the action? The time itself was very uncondusive, he didn't have a bit trust upon any one, neither of law nor of officers. Still, he with little expectation had entered into the campus of police station. He usually doesn't have any fear of police station or of court, being a lawyer. There were two men were sitting on dais in covering themselves, not known clearly where they were dozing or not? 'May be sufferers like us', He thought. The head police was on duty outside and inside, the second officer and two to three sub-ordinate police constables were there. On the yard some people were there. On the yard, some people were hurry in search of pen and paper and lawyer to write an FIR. He dirted hand in the pocket and brought out a coin of five rupees to buy papers. Rajani Pradhan had opened the staff there and started to write 'Respected Dear', they asked to the accused, tell the problems."

He overheard the report called by names while he was standing there. He felt that all of them were suffering from the incidents. The theme of all applications, perhaps was same : The intruded hundred in number were armed with the weapons in their hands, looted everything and arsoned the houses and beat hard to all. They had requested for drastic action against the accused.

Is there any action takes place? He grumbled with that ancient thoughts. If, its seen, there were thousands of names of the accused, if total no of accused are aided one after another. How long that cases will continue for final decisions?

What a really useful of writing them, "Esteemed sir?" Nothing happens there and nothing will happen. He was just coming back towards camp. The scene of unknown persons flashed upon his eyes, he proceeded towards them to recognise them. They were father and daughter sitting there. They even dare not taking to each other.

"Have you collected a copy of the FIR, that had lodged in the police station?" He asked.

The man was sitting wrapped a bed sheet like a shawl-sheet by half opened head just nodded his head. I think, I should give an FIR, but I have no money to pay for the FIR's writer. His residence is Rudangia and named Christdas Nayak. Both father and daughter had nothing with them except the cloth and shawl but all had turned up ashes in fire.

"I have pen and paper, you may take and write a report in it. He brought out a piece of paper from his bag of portfolio. But Christdas let out his bandaged right hand to take that paper and took into the sheet again.

They had broken out his hands. He amazed and sympathetic. Yes! Let me write, you dictate.

Christiadas began, "Esteemed Dear one"

He just checked him, well! Let me know, "Do you think, these Mr Dears will give us justice."

"Who knows, if there will be any action?" why should I bother about that, I need the copy of an FIR. I will preserve that throughout my life. Whenever I need, I could read that. That piece of paper of the report will keep me energetic.

How the oppression can imbalance the mind of

person, he was reading on the face of Christdas. His daughter was peeping with glimmering eyes. The lips were dried up to wet any word.

Here, there are three relief camps, in which one you stay with. Till now, I am in where, I have come here for writing a report after the work is over, I will go away.

Where will you stay? Perhaps in relatives house. All my relatives have turned up ashes. We both the father and daughter will leave this place. Not to any particular place but wherever we desire.

Then what will be the use of these FIR?

Wherever we may go no matter, but we have to leave this report here. Only to let them remember that we were born in this place. We have lost everything, we will not stay – Did we have ever here?

There was no fear in gruel eyes of Christdas Nayak. He was breathing hard. Otherhand his family was waiting for him in the camp. He hurried up. He thought, were the words of a single application change one's mind? Oh may be, at any time – He answered it with that letter in his hand "lets proceed", asked his daughter.

Dear,

The IIC, Police Station, G-Udaygiri

Sir,

I Sri Christdas Nayk, age 55, S/o- Janakrushna Nayak Residence – Rudangia, PS – G-Udaygiri, Dist.-Kandhamal. I would like to produce this report before your majesty that Nage Prusty S/o- Bhimaraj Prusty, Bhimsen Pradhan S/o- Boda Pradhan, Laxman Acharya S/o- Patitapaban Acharya, Natabar Panda S/o- Satyabadi Panda of G-Udaygiri town had invaded the adjacent villages Rudangia and Ganjabuda and other villages simultaneously and took an attempt to kill people and arsons houses on 30.09.2008. Last day, i.e., on 29.09.2008 I myself, my wife, daughter were sitting on the yard and watching the house. Today morning i.e. on 30.09.2008, almost one thousand people armed with violent weapons had surrounded our villages. They set fire my house. Sanjib Pradhan of Pandhagada village slabbed with the harpoon at the ear of my wife when she opposed him doing that mischief. When she fell down, Bamadev Pradhan of our village hewed the neck with bill hock and Nehamani Pradhan of Pandhagada with an axe at her back and Pande Pradhan and Babaji Pradhan beat her hard with sticks. All limbs of my wife cut into pieces. Blood streamed from her head. We, both father and daughter couldn't save her life. Then all the accused set fire in Lebaguda, Kunjuguda, Padeguda, Jomaguda villages. They broke all the home appliances. All, Gopal Pradhan, Suramati Pradhan, Rulu Nayak, Houre Nayak, Abinash Nayak, Iasini Nayak, Mandakini Nayak, Lazi Nayak, Satapathy Nayak, Junesh Nayak were bathed in blood. They are at danger. The accused did not care for the presence of the police officer rather engaged them in devastation. My wife died due to sever injury in body.

This is for your information and necessary action.

Yours faithfully,

Christdas Nayak

His hand, writing report for Christdas trembled in fear. He had saved his life and came rushing but he had lost everything there. He feels himself Christdas. As if the same sorts of reactions in him, he could feel.

Christdas, as if had wrapped the wound of the funeral pyre of his wife.

A signature was needed at the end of the application.

The left hand under the wrap of cloth, he let's out, and took the pen and put the signature in zigzag stroke of handwriting.

FOLK LIVES

I, not for all times, usually for sometimes, sleep on the leaf of Salap tree. I dream that forest, bald hills and many. I dream them marching in procession to graveyard beneath the narrow bushy path of danger hills. They are always accompanied by diseases, tiger, rain and other calamities. I think someone is died either of diseases or by tiger's attack and they are carrying the dead body of that man. I hark their lamented song.

> O' great God!
> God is above.
> Dartarni-Earth underneath
> We all greet you
> Beesch you
> Today one of us has passed away
> Of our kith and kin,
> Of our family
> Someone has forgotten the track
> Someone to derailed
> With our forefathers
> With our sacred forefathers
> We unite all'f them
> To live together
> To merry make with each other

> Let there be no hindrances
> In their returned journey
> We the lived people
> We live here
> May we live healthy and happy lives
> Our cattle mother
> Our giver of livelihood
> Let they increase grow
> Let ourselves free from
> Disease, sorrow, pain and strain
> Let our homes, roads
> Forest, hills, rivers and valley
> Be in proper state
> Juhar Juhar Juhar
> We pay regards honour
> And respects.

They all were proceeding shouting Juhar Juhar. The sound was unheard, disappeared in cul-de-sac. The voice of their great song was shallowed by the densities of forest. I got up galvanised from the salap leave. It was already morning.

They usually pass the preview of day's affairs. They make themselves busy in climbing the hills, coming down of hills till the set of the san in the western horizon as their direction. They cultivate the Danger and the patches beneath the danger too during day time.

The works almost all times in the fields such as Suan, Alasi, Kandula and the weed out piri grass from them never end. They never confine themselves in works, rather they got up from work to have a round at Jhola Kula bandha to hunt mule and moved towards cooked Madha. Some Dhangda leave the work place to have a ramble in village.

The smell of cooked rice-Beheri-mandu and curry of tamarind addition and leni ambada spread all over the village.

I came down from salap tree and sat on the shoulder of a Dhangda. I whispered in slow voice, in the voice not to be heard to the wind-let us see what is walking beneath the Danger?

That antic young man looked fumbled and felt foolish looked towards corn fields beneath the Danger. He fumbled and felt foolish what ever thing came upon. I swimmed in the wind and left the place and went to sit on a stone upon Danger.

There were five people in the cultivated land caps on heads. They were measuring something here and there. Someone was observing with a machine closed it. The machine stood on three-legged stand. Others were waving their hands. And other two were measuring land with tape. The ripped crops were waving golden tide. But they were least concerned with ripped crops rather stampeding them.

That Dhanga shouted to let others inform about stampeding of crops beneath the Danger field. Are they sycophant of zamindars or Amin of Government? Some of farmers left the field to take rest under the tree and were drinking Mandia Jurum, podding. Krushna Saunta was smoking dhungia in chirut of Sialli leave. He got annoyed and his blood boiled out of anger viewing such type of activities and mischief in crop field.

Akhila Saunta is our MLA. He is present in village. Let us go to him to know the truth. All the people: Maharaj, Laxman, Postmaster Majhi, Shyamaghana, Subhas Dhangada, Akhila, Bhagaban Majhi, Suresh, Ghusura, Tanga Vidya, Bangaru at the call of Krushna Saunta. Lachhama, Premi, Pamu, Russo, Anchla, Mami, Ambai, Tuni and Alli, all maiji dhangdis accompanied by them. All stood gathered in front of the building of Akhila Saunta.

Akhila Saunta had put on a napkin-Gamuchha and was washing the shed of buffalos. He never likes to stay at Bhubaneswar except during Assembly session. He finds his native place Kacheripadara more comfortable than the capital city Bhubaneswar.

Akhila Saunta listened everything and smiled.

"Go, Go to your fields. The Government has sent them to measure lands. Your lands will be developed. Don't afraid of that." the MLA spoke to them.

They all ignited at the consolation of the MLA. Just after three or four days later - they are the people of strange obstinacy. Tikira is just three to four kilometres distance from village. They all carried cement pillars for pointer of the lands. MLA has assured them for the development of their lands. It's government's decision. They all-embedded cement pillars in their lands. They don't have fear of anything: cultivation, drinking of Mahuli, flattering of Dhangda Dhangdi with each other and domestic works. They all remain busy in preparation of forthcoming festival-paraba for dance, song etc.

I was sitting on a stonefloor in middle of the river. I could not digest the statement of Akhila Saunta.

Kandha people never tell lie. Why did Akhila Saunta speak lie? I tried to motivate my obstinate thoughts. Yes, Akhila Saunta is no more a man of Kandha. He has become a Malhara, a richman, a hench man of government and captivated by vote and politics.

They all made themselves busy in preparation of Puspunei drama. People of different parts of the village, beginning from middle to end part of the village wear gathered to watch the play. The play began. One of the dhangdas was playing the role of RI and other one was acting as his peon. Who was playing comic role by saying the comical and numerous dialogues to make the audience laugh. "You have a lot of landed property. Give Sisthu, the tax."

Some of the audiences were actors. They must have collected nine Sukhila, dried fish, kandul dal and rats with great difficulties. They all will pay sisthu, the tax to the RI sir. If the payment is found low payment, immediately RI will react to it. And he will instruct the peon for punishment of the less payer. The peon will beat him with the straw kuncle duster. The Dhangdis will roll on the ground viewing such false whipping of the Dhangdas. What a laugh of the Dhangdies!

Then RI sir declare I got sisthu. Share the sisthu. Then fire is set. All collected fifty or forty rats are put in the fire to let burn, capsicum dust added to them to make the dish tasty. They shared Kandul dal, fried fish, sukhua, rats etc. collected from tax. The rich Saunta took one share. The cow herd took one part, the barber, barika took another share. Then song and dance performance began.

I entered into the programme of song and dance. I sat on the shoulder of a Dhangda, within that dance programme by round the hands. And told in slow voice in his ear look who is that man approaching. The dance of that dhangda became disturbed. He made others conscious to behold the scene! Someone is coming. All the sounds of the song and dance stopped to see the stranger. All had paid their attention to stranger.

The stranger had a spectacle in his eyes. He wore a criss cross strip banian and an leather bag under his armpit.

"I'm from Agragami."

What is this Agragami? The early speaker, Krushna

Saunta asked in advance. In return of that Agragami man imposed subscription on Krushna Saunta. Let us go to salap tree I will explain you everything there.

That stranger sat on the soil under the salap tree of Krushna Saunta. Maharaj and Laxman Majhi reached there. Krushna climbed the tree and downed the salap dumbi-pot to ground. When the four were intoxicated Jhumi Jhami, the Agragami man stood to speak them - 'Agragami is a reputed social organisation. Achyuta Das, an educated young man had come to this district Kasipur before ten to twelve years. In those days it was neither cycle nor any vehicle could possible to run on this path. He moved from village to village accompanied by some young people.

They made aware of people. They literated them. Distributed medicine for disease free of cost. This Agragami organisation stands for the prosperity of the people. We have decided to start work in your village for your development.

I was dozing sitting in one place. My sleep was interrupted by his speech. I got myself present without knowledge of others.

That man suggested, who would shoulder the responsibility of Agragami organisation for your village? We have lot of works to do in your village. We provide a lot of opportunities for you. We will provide you allowance and take you on Delhi tour.

I was observing the man intended to open organisations only in tribal areas. I was watching his activities and waiting for the man who would take that responsibilities of the organisation.

We all three are government servants. How could we take the responsibilities of your organisation?

Laxman Majhi is the man of responsibility. He spoke this in advance and other two just nodded their heads in support of Laxman Majhi. The Agragami man did not pay any attention at the plea of them. He told, you're Laxman Majhi, Maharaj Majhi is a govt. teacher. You Krushna Saunta a fourth-grade employee of the irrigation department just nominally. The irrigation department incessantly dormant here. Why will you sleep inactively. 'Awake! do some work for your people.' These two friends of yours will cooperate you in work. You Krushna Saunta take the responsibility of the organisation, the Agragami man suggested.

Laxman and Maharaj Majhi proposed, 'let it be so'. That man of Agragami set out his journey before evening. These three got up to the road to see off him. Shyamghana, Suvas, Bhagaban Majhi followed them. Before he drove the cycle, he stopped for a moment.

Be aware, and be conscious, a great danger has risen its head for these areas.

"What type of danger?"

Laxman Majhi, like a humble student, enquired to know about the danger.

The Hawk is flying over your land, river, forest and Danger. See you again. I will narrate everything under that salap tree.

That man of Agragami had left the place riding the bicycle. Since long the search of the hawks in the sky was still captivated them in the clouds where that hawk is flying over? How large and big Hawk would be? From what distance that hawk would come up? They imagined many things about the hawks.

The darkness of the night has spread over from the surrounding hills : A diapabuli, Sullamals, Lekdamka. Just at the time, the banging sound of Dhemsa Drum was heard. That was the day of get together, Jantala, a grand feast before the chitagudi goddess, Thakurani presiding under the Sal tree. One can eat as much as one needs that Mandia-rice, wine and Ambidi etc. All the Dhangda and Dhangdi came out of huts being heard the banging sound of Dhemsa. Then started the song and dances.

There was amusements of song and dance in front of Chitagudi, whereas, others were in search of Hawks in the sky in other side. This foolishness made me laugh. I took myself to the shoulder of a man and whispered in his ear with slow voice, let us move to Chitagudi Thakurani. They had forgotten the hawks flapping sound and looking into the sky and came to function and indulged themselves in song and dance till late night.

Next day, I was sleeping downward on Kada of the river of a flat stone in evening. I was waving my hands in river water to get the fish up and think about the date of observation of Gadhapuja. All will come to the river jetty. Disari, the priest will sacrifice cock. They will recollect the old tradition. All these seven sisters have turned up Duma. After sacrifice of cock, they will let that seven sisters get up from water bed and the Dumas will let the fish arise to up. They will catch fish as much as they need.

I dip my hands in water to let the fish up. I remain busy in unnecessary works. I didn't have time to watch if the moon was blooming in the sky or not that day. The postmaster Majhi was trotting over the bridge like Rafkana towards village. He was painting and anxious to put down the burden of news that he carried in his mind before the people of his village to get himself relaxed. I painted after him bobbing the darkness.

Postmaster Majhi came upon Atanu just at entering into village. They sat down on the high pucca yard of Laxman Majhi. Then Krushna and Maharaj joined them later.

Postmaster Majhi put down that news from his

breast. Anataram Majhi, the leader of the opponent party passing comments at the people of our village: you will die! Wait. You all tribal Kandha wait and see what happens. Your parental lands, and cultivated lands all will go, will be snatch away from you. Company is arriving very soon.

Company who is he? All were sitting silently. This news was spread all over the village before midnight. Company... company.

As if everything was changed next day. People began to converse different type of words. All that happiness disappeared on the face of every and each man. When Suvas Majhi was sowing earthen pot Mandia, Kandul, Khangel seed in Kadaka, he spoke all about that company before Suresh Lachhama has kept engaged the beloved Dhangdis Maijis at Kada ghat with company matter. The news about company was discussed among the people at the place of cooking of wine, Chitagudi Thakurani, Goddess, drinking of podding and Jurum, fedding the Poda buffalos. Preparation of Dhangia smoke of under the salap tree. A common talk about the arrival of company had the villager's hot in conversation.

People's prediction and assumption went up high in different versions. A dhangda told his friend: company is a demon. It will shallow our dungers and inhabitation. A film viewer dhanda compared company with a villain of a film, may be bigger than him. Everybody: police, Headu, Forester, Garudu and RI all scare of him.

I observe how the dance and song and merrymaking of all that pleasant moments all have vanished on their faces. A dhangda, standing on his cultivated land asked, is this land mine?

They don't have interest in cultivation, tilling, business, services and jobs. So, to say in no work. Some of them had given up the thought of company and made them busy in cultivation obstinately.

People shouted on company. Air revolted against company. The man of Agragami arrived on the spot at right time.

Intimacy of the Agragami man had gone deep with Krushna Saunta. He understood, the people of that village has shown their interest for Agragami organisation. Some dhangdas, maiji, dhangdi all are becoming intimate with this organisation. Lovers of Lachhami are growing with this organisation. This time people are paying him regards uttering Ajna, Ajna and stand around him.

I was present there. I flew to the shoulder of a dhangda and whispered at his ear in low voice, company.

O the dhangda excited and asked to that man of Agragami, if he could know about the company.

Let us go to beneath the salap tree, I will explain.

I am ashamed of these types of tendency of the outsider. They always have eyes on Tribal Kandha's lovable things. After drank of salap, the man sat hearing against the salap tree. All looked at his face with great expectation.

This company is actually nothing but it has a lot of things to do. This style of answer in model of coastal belt people made the understanding of our people mysterious. Laxman Majhi got irritated: please tell clearly.

It is a multinational company by the joint venture of Hydro Aluminium company of Norway and Tata Indul company of India both have made an international Ltd. Company. They will excavate Buxite from your Baflimali mountain and set up Alumina factory at Dora of your village.

If they dig the mine and set up factory, we the people what to do with them. Do they do any harm to us? That Agragami man told to that   dhangda by showing his fore finger, that company will displace you to other places.

Neither your forest, nor your water, nor your lands nor your habitants, nothing will have any existence after it.

Four arrows were shut on the breast of that people gathered there.

"Lands, forests, water and we ourselves where shall we go?"

Agragami man got up from the jag of salap. He just gave a hints, "If you desire you can stay here, at the time of parting to Kasipur. We will stay here too."

The moon had just peeped out her face behind the Sualimali hill. But no radiance was seen on the face of anyone. They all moved like shadows into the lane one after another. I chased after their shadows as another shadow.

I climbed up to the brown soft sprouted twings of sal tree. Well! What will happen to them now? Could I able to stay here? All these complicated questions raised in my mind, they overcrowd my thoughts, I fumble, I dozed.

The company of England comes in my dream. She digs the Baflimali hill. Baflimali disappeared in a moment. Sterlite Company comes to the Niyamgiri hill, there is no mark of inhabitation. Larcen Company comes, no mark of the Sijimalli hill or the Kutumali hill, all disappeared in twinkle of eye blinking. Alcon company of America come as well as Aditya Birla and Hindul come too. Many companies of different varieties. They have hanged their boards and shared the entire places among themselves. Asphalt roads are under construction. The logs of sail and piasals are rolling on the ground. The vehicles of foreign companies are running in the areas emitting smoke. The heavy cargo, trollies are carrying giant like machines: Bulldozer, crane for plants day and night. Now I see and it appears to my eyes how is there no mark of habitation of Singaram, Balimodi Srungar of three villages, the places look desert. Quarters of lower-paid employees are under construction. Aditya Birla is connecting electricity to that place. Bungalows for officers are constructed separately. 2/2 quarters and apartments are constructed for labour class people. I observe how the three villages, Panjali, Barigan and Letiput have been submerged in water. The Dam is constructed above them. Aditya Birla is connecting electricity from that Dam to his plant. The Railway lines are under construction to link them from mines area to plant site. The stations are standing there. Haripur village has been replaced by Helipad. The small Air buses are lifting people of different languages, colours of different ground, space for Night Clubs are hurriedly constructed. I listen the melody of song, music and dance flowing from the club and jag. I do not find any mark of people of this village. Where were they gone. I see half of the population have left since long. I see the misfortune of the people. Some people were on footpath, some are to sale themselves in red lite area like an offering to the Gods. The rest of them stayed here to serve in the company in the rank of peon, gardener, cook and in different jobs. Some dhangdis are working in the quarters and bungalows of officers as caretaker of child or as Nariani to clear the remnant utensils or in cleaning the marble floors etc. and the old people and Maijis are made themselves busy in sweeping the roads, cleaning the latrine tanks and drains. The dhangdas are working in factory like machines. The furosis disease has broken out and spread widely in slum area and labour colonies. The rest of the villagers are dying like insects in my village.

I see, there is not a single drop of water in the river Nagabali. No trace of the Bansadhara, the Indrabati. The source of fountains, hills and Kajagada are dried up. Scarcity of drinking water arised. The poison of fluoride has been spread in everything. Sheep, buffalo-podha, dogs, cats all are drinking this fluoride water. Their bones are bending automatically in effect of this reaction. The domestic species of animals are slowly on the process of extinct.

I turned my body up in sleeping for comfort. Everything turned in blinking of eyes. I reached the time after thirty years. The scene after thirty years appeared to my eyes. I predict. All will leave this place and all are hurry for this. First the officers left this place accompanied by their families and followed by the lower-class employees. Once the place which was crowded by people and bazars, all are leaving the place one after another. The truck and trollies are carrying giant size machines of the plants. Quarters remain vacant. Trains, busses become over crowded, as all are hurry to leave the place. All bauxites after excavation was processed and shifted to other places. The village became empty only pits. All the mineral products are no more under the earth. There is no worth of the place.

I looked all around, all the houses looked useless like phantom sheds, haunts. Railway compartments are falling derailed and rusted unused. Aqua trees-weeds have grown in swimming pools. The asphalt, pucca roads turned rugged and looked like previous muddy roads. Heaps of rags are piled here and there. Unused product of the factory stands like poisoned pillar. The atmosphere if filled with carbon dioxide and sulphur and their aftermath effects. Acid rain poured down on empty inhabitation.

I got perished in that acid rain. I have seen, the company people replaced the native men. They also left this place after thirsty years. Why I am here? A Duma (ghost) without people has no use to stay here. No difference between staying.

I just sobbing for my existencelessness. I heard someone was coughing beneath the tree. I got up from slumber that broken dreams disappeared completely. I looked under the tree passionately. Nothing was changed there till that time. Native people were there. Their conversations was heard. Three men were sitting on Benarmunda, the meeting place of the tribe. Maharaja Majhi was suffering from TB and coughing continuously. Laxman Majhi was talking very substantially. Krushna Saunta was preparing dhungia in siali leave and tobacco leave's dust silently. When the talk was about Lachhaman, he shallowed spite. On the other hand Lachhaman was his in relation. At the same time Krushna can't stay without Lachhaman. Lachhaman was agree to leave her own male and live with Krushna Saunta. When she was dhangda, you could not bring her, she went with another male. If she comes to you, you will have to be alienated from the clan. You will have to leave the village.

He sconced the dhungia in ear. Folded his hands. Cried like a child. I can't leave this village.

This matter would have been discussed till late night I came rushing from the bed of sal leaves. I whispered at the ears of Laxman Majhi 'Forest and Land'.

First Laxman became conscious. The blood of Krushna Saunti got hot. Will this land of forefathers, be with us? Will this forest be with us tomorrow? Will the problem of water arise? Where should we be? Yes, the complicacies, the unsolved problems, work out of the sum for tomorrow went on discussed.

Krushna Saunti hitted the store of Benamunda with his fists aggressively.

Kandhas talks the present. But these three Kandhas were shouting for tomorrow's problem.

Let the darkness be not waved. I stood behind their shadows. I lifted myself to the shoulder of Krushna Saunti. I whispered at his ear, 'We will fight."

HALF A MAN

Hey Nonsense Laxman, puppy of a beech, if the hot midday alive in slum, there is intoxication in the brain of this Murmu. The entire fourteen world appear before him. Only one face is visible to him. He has not made the mask of wooden frames so far. Therefore, he picks up a muddy puppy to his lap and named it Laxman. Then scolding and quarrel are both inter crossed. If Laxman reached on the spot accidentaly, then Murmu fumble, word failed to utter, shrinked out of shame by himself. And dropped the puppy from his clutch and leave that on the ground. Unnecessarily, dissuaded the puppy by scolding him.

Father afraid of a son, after drinking of Handia. The son scared of father, returned by drunk of foreign liquor.

Murmu is adept in drinking of Malmula. He has started drinking of Handia since he was twenty one day's of his life. Now the daringness of shaking the forest has become slow down or Lento. His lips and throat are dried up after drunk. In place of go for hunting with Arrow and bow and dance by banging drum Madal, the intoxication has made him sat in one place. The name Murmu is understood by suspicion, doubt, inability and suffering of impotency.

His son in search of a job has tried to be ousted from forest. Now-a-days he works in Nilagiri and hardly does work either for one or two days, go for cinema and returned money by coins and drunk. He see the entire village is drinking country wine from the contractor. Nothing is there in the forest. Drinking wine quickly and vomiting just after it, means disappearance of intoxication. He is very young Laxman. Little drunk make him much intoxication. Bangan means Bangan. Banga - useless for no work obstinate for that land Bhumja - quick for explanation.

What did you tell? I'm puppy - what are you then? Aren't you dog?

How can I be dog? Does the dog ask his mother? (Kukur kia pachare tora Ma'ke!)

This word shot like arrow to his wife's heart. Mother knows the mystery of her child's birth. If anyone comments to that mystery, a mother bites him. She roars like tigress and ordered to stops that hue and cry. She supported Murmu's argument. His wife was shouting and making hue and cry. Her anger vibrating the earth and sky with curse.

As the daily wagers accept the rosa without any hesitation. Does the same daily wagers who have never been to outside for wages accept the Rosa. As if this conflict has been arisen in between his father and mother. Since his date of birth the attack and counter attack taking place for which she neither sleeps nor awake in bed rather the remain awake in the state of half toxication and humiliation. The five macabre masks made from big wood logs have been reclined against the wall. All that have been made by his father. All that masks made by his father appended to him like magic in half drowsy and toxication. If one mask's nose look bigger then there is no mouth of other mask at all. One side of the mask look human but other half look very peculiar. Whereas the stone eyes have been set in improper place of one mask.

The stone eyed mask drew his attention and cohered.

As if a diamond dazzling-transparent has been hidden under the white stone. If one looks without seriousness that mask appear very common. That eyes appear glittering in darkness like the eyes of a witch, Katyayeeni. He frightened and fainted before that eyes. No alternative strikes to his mind but confused. He fails to understand why his wastrel father lathe the logs to make masks? Why he decorate them home like temple.

The power of intoxication come down slowly in midday. But the sensitiveness overcrowded his mind. There was meaningless quarrel was taking place in the yard uselessly. Someone stands with an axe and threaten, "I will cut you - end you."

Silence prevailed everywhere. He threw the Axe away distance. He pulled himself out from the slum to the midway. Jungle stands two sides of the path. Hills stand silently like shadow in little distance. The musical sounds of drum, madala, drim… drim… blow floating from the lanes of hills. Some tribal women, Tirla and males are carrying cocks in arms and toodi, Handia wine on head were going to distant market. He made himself relaxed recline against the Mahula tree.

There is no work either in Nilagiri, or in Balasore or in Seragarh, nowhere nearby places. Here the rosa, the daily wagers of Balasore, Mayurbhanja and local people all make crowded this place. Humn! Cuttack means Cuttack, say about the place or about the availability of works, very nice from all points of view. Young people of your age have earned too much Tukuli money and they are enjoying their lives. You are strong, straight and stout like a sal tree, what will you do staying in village?

He matches his thoughts with the expression of the broker - grumbled actually nothing is there in this village.

He always set his mind up to travel to a new place. Before he see off the place, first he went rushing to the market place to drop all his experiences - nostalgia and enjoyment he had lived in village. It is usual meeting with tokli-girls, both known and unknown readymade stationaries there. Big market place is always hue and cry everywhere. It gives him a feeling of deserted life, family, shopping, graveyard all these have no meaning without money. He may be a man alive or dead.

It is usually sleeping that never comes to his eyes. I slept flat looking upward with half closed eyes. If there is a little sound of hen under the basket, he turned the body up. The masks are before his eyes swayed in swing. He himself is alone before him. He becomes spooky like children out of fear. He gropes for parents in thick gloominess. Murmu was snoozing in deep sleep. It was betel dribbling from corner of the mouth. His mother was sleeping nude in other corner of the room. Her half grey Karanja massaged hairs fall scattered on the ground.

He hides his face to the slept dormant parents. He hides his face to the masks. Though he slept downward but he had no despite from the masks. They made him dance both inside and outside, disturbed him, all that eyes of stone mask.

Now this is the turn of the stone eyes. He takes decision. Morning descended on the earth. Father went to village to smoke pika and for gossip. Mother went to forest for collecting brush stick and collecting dab etc. He walked to bazar in search of a goldsmith shop. He gathered strength to enter into shop. He opened the waist nut find package. Then he found that stone eyes to fetch the goldsmith. Look at this lord stones my. "What type of stone is it? How much will it be?"

Through that thick powered spectacle, the gold smith assayed the material through that stone as well as read the psychology of the customer. He threw that stone eyes to the front roads, just to divert the attention of the customer. He let the customer give that stone that he brought with him. This stone is worthless and not at all fit to be the stone for a ring.

Laxman runs to the road crying to pick up that stone eyes from road and stands before the goldsmith with supplication. That Goldsmith tells sympathetically, Hey! Try to give up the habit of Adivasi's attitude. You the people, you're very obstinate. Are the valuable precious metals available in the hills of Balasore and Mayurbhanj? But they are usually available in Kalahandi and Balangir. Have you stolen this stone from elsewhere. His integrity is questioned - why should I steal? My landlord sir. This is my own.

Okay. You take ten to fifteen rupees. If you have brought, give me. However I will manage it. That shop keeper called him. He remain in to be and not to be condition. Whether to transact or not. The shopkeeper bargain the cost. Take twenty five rupees. He brought from his land to leave the place. But shopkeeper hopes, that he will never go but told. If you don't like you may go. Leave it, now take round fifty rupee. Give it."

He could understand the trick and about the quality of the stone as the cost of it was hiking in hands of this Goldsmith. How much would if be if it is sold? Where shall he go with that money? Again he came back and put the stone eye in the place of that mask where he took to sale that and felt relaxed after putting that in its own place.

He needs a victory to forget these things, A fighting, a revolution. He took off and brought down arrow and bow from ceiling. Dust fell upon him. He pulled cubes of arrow.

He tested the strength of that cubes and its hardness. That will be the last prey of him in the village. He ran rushing into forest like storm an obstinate man. As if the things of unsuccessfulness was written in the fate, the sound being heard out of stepping on dried leaves. There was no trace of fowl or dear nearby. It was only trees and forest, his only thirst and desire but there was the silence calm and quite everywhere.

He searched for earth pot wine, 'Handia' when he reached at village. Intoxication was multiplied, then he needs dance and drum. That earthen pot wine is always available without any fast and festivals in tribal villages. Keke bangs drum. No dance without group.

Not easy to enter into the house at once. Murmu was engraving the wood log to make lower part of the eyes, the pick of the nose, border of the ears and last portion of the forehead of the statue. Father can understand the intoxication of son out of imbalanced walking steps. Murmu scolded him in humming voice of bees. If one collect firewood and make sal leaves cups or collect honey, he will earn money. Nonsense, forest smells him rotten. He laughs shamelessly hearing this grumbling. He never miss that retaliation in response to his father's grumbling. What're you doing? "Or tui kisa karuchu?" Why do you stock all that masks in rooms instead of selling them? We will have some money.

Hey nonsense, son of pigs. Watch! they are made from wood. These are our own look out. That is the mask of big nose, he is my father's father - great witch craft (witch-doctor). He was so skilled that he could make the hill walk and make the trees disappear. He has eaten up his own wife - tirla. This house has been famed after his name but father has sold up everything. He sold all the cultivated lands but died left the house unsold. And the mask having no trace mouth may be of my father. And that single mouth shaped mask is of mine. Saying this and narrating these masks, "Murmu was laughing like stupid. Have you seen me? - "Mute tui dekhichu nare?" I having sitted idle like one eyed man, your mother became Reja - a daily wager and sponsored everything for your father. She has managed me by selling the stick bundle of toothbrush. The stone-eyed mask must be your mother's. My father's father has collected that stone from the Meghasan Hill. I have made her witch craft by wearing that mask (Sei take mar mukha lagei mui take bandari kari rakhichi). Had she not bound she would have been escaped since long.

His explanation was yet to over. Murmu's wife comes out immoderation. What berate could be used for the man having a concubine of his own. The anger thrashing of feet, expression of excitement reflect his impotency of his own. Usual tendency of all human beings. You nonsense, with a voice of threat, would you stop this making of mask or not? (Tui gata pasa mukha gadha band karibu na nai.) With action of anger, I will throw them out, burn you out, turn you ashes, be aware of it.

All these abusive is useless for the man like him who is making mask, passionately. He smiles at the attitudes of his wife. She becomes more infarious, mode, vendictive. Look at my work Tirla. This mask is made for Laxman. I won't make the ears of this mask. He would hear, had he the ears - the ears of your son. Difficult to know the man of which species.

He does all these things inside the room. She goes rushing threatening to Murmu. Murmu's skeleton becomes active. He holds the throat of his mother. Doubts, suspension, anger enranged themselves to get angry with each other. But he come out of home and stand on the road. Deep dark had spread like mist upto Sergarh Chauk. Agent, broker, catching vehicle and works at Cuttack.

Its morning, the first step of the day. The broker take him upto labour camp. He experienced the feeling of chous in Cuttack. The women workers, Reja are from Keonjhar, Andapur area. No one was there of his area. The entire days are spent digging soil and rights give them rest and eating in their company. He, in the eyes of others, as if is the alien man, but they are sons of the soil. They all satire him in their conversation. The more joke is done by Keonjhar, Reja. They all drink country wine, Handia but don't forget calling him Kaptipada, Kaptipada.

The half made mask comment him, "You are the son of a Reja, a daily wager woman, what more could you expect doing this work. As if the stone eyed mask sweep hands on his sleepy back, and saying that every work is important and has certain value. May not at Kaptipada but at Cuttack. Wherever you stay. Stay happy.

The work of spreading of cable wires ended by contractors job. The temporary camp removed to other place. All the workers, along with their groups go back to their own village or search for otherwork. The broker is not available at right time of the chouk of Shergad. Daily wagers in number ten like him, enter into town for work. If he goes back home, then again to return to errand all his income will be finished. Had he the family, he would have a thought of savings.

I'm zero, empty, nothing is there even to manage myself. Early in the morning with certain hope, I sit on Bajrakabati Road. Sanjaya cafee restura in one side and the sweet stall of Gouranga Sahoo in opposite direction. Both sides of the roads are the market place for daily wagers. There was heavy crowds of daily wagers from Keonjhar, Mayurbhanja, Balasore, Berhampur, Dhenkanal. I found a mansion was surrounded. Then quarrel begins among the mansions.

Firstly, he was engaged to dig soil for foundation of the construction. The work promoted to help the mansion to mix cement, with granite stone and sand and supply to mansion, the works proceed step by step, but I couldn't concentrate at errand. The day, he holds trowel to assist the mansion for plastering, he feels himself half-mansion, and finds much comfort with pride. He takes a care of putting the bricks one after another in proper order and fill the gaps with trowel mixed sand and cement. No tribal mansion has never allowed a tribal labour to catch the plumb and trowel in construction work what he does today. They never let the tribal labour proceed with other works. Sometimes he doesn't feel comfort in labour work.

If he finds overtime works, day after that he doesn't go to labour market for work. He decides a day for him. He goes to movie and drinks with friends, if any one comes to him, then returned to his temporary inhabitants in drowsiness and numbness pain. The thought of impossibilities, if he could avail a job tomorrow or not, still, he remembers the sensation of blowing of spasmodic breeze on the bank of Kathajodi, the uncertainty of getting a work always chase after him. The real life runs in frustration and intoxication but dream move speedily on bicycle and that cycle of fiction carries a carrier made up of motor tyre having all the equipment of mansion in it. Trowel, Batli, borer, chisel, saw, balance, saw-cutter, plumb and so on. Yes! It is very easy to become a mansion of imagination. It is an old city, Cuttack, being coiled by the Mohanadi and the Kathajodi on both sides but the middle is jammed by concrete buildings. There is not a space for a man to put his head in, who cares a daily wagers for here.

Once, he came upon, aman of distance relations from the area of Baisinga, who enquires about his wellbeing. He is found to be very much eager and emotional to open the Chatter-box, about the experiences of outside places, before a close person like him. Works and its availability is scanty in this city. Tomorrow can't be predicted from today and todays earning is ended today, no surplus for tomorrow. Rather, he suggests the return back to Kaptipada again. His feelings of impatience is consoled by that relatives. He told, all the jobs of Cuttack are moving rapidly towards Bhubaneswar. Would you like to go to Bhubaneswar?

After a long gap, a feeling stroke to his thought, as if two trees were engaged in conversation.

I think, I should touch the village, the village scenes, people and manythings have preoccupied his mind. He will decide, after parting of relatives but he can't but things to go fast to Kaptipada. He will think, after returned, whether, he will hult at Kaptipada or drop at Cuttack or at Bhubaneswar, still all my thoughts remain undecided.

The felt the smell of fragrance of his own soil in semi-darkness of evening after got down at Kaptipada - muddy, muddy soft soft footpath. He fumbled, why has he come to village? Has he come being drawn by the affection of parents or to prove his eligibility of being a he man?

The surrounding forests make a face, and asks what the matter Mr. Laxman? As if they make a point and asks, "Laxman you are fed up with village, she has nothing, where have you come now?"

The crematory ground, passed by, all the suppressed fear that I did have and that heard from the ancestors were hanging like spiders wave around my heart. The earthen pots given food to the dead person on tenth day of death were reflecting, better to say glittering in moon beam. Such fearness, trembled me, but the name of village Goddess idol, all of a sudden came rushing to mind. The visibility of the idol was shadowed by the denseness of sal trees. All but the cocks and hens were awaken except others. Everything reflects silhouette prints of shadow and light, and painted to the footpath.

He knocked, slowly on his own door. Open the door. I'm Laxman; the door, without his knowledge, just opened with friction. He could not understand now did he come and stand under the dropping thatched yard and when her cracked and dusty folding palm picked up his foreign returned face and had rested her head on the bony breast with great cry. She took him into the lap of darkness. She was not Murmu but his mother.

Just before he left home, all of sudden he fell ill and slashed in stool and urine in ailing state, even did not keep cloth in body, and remain busy in scolding the wife who was in her father's home and working as daily wager, Reza and was cursing the son working outside as daily wager, Murmu was living with these activities. At last his hands were paralysed and the mask remain incomplete.

He stood like orphan before the half finished mask of Murmu, in which he would not keep ears in the son's mask. He did not but make no ear in the son's mask. There was up in construction of nose and mouth was plain, eyes of the wood looked large and eye lids and below were still uncurved, a half-made mask of Laxman. Nothing was new to him for the villagers and sympathy for him was beyond his thought. The son of witch craft, Murmu died. A problem solved, it was only this youngman remain alive in that family. All were fed up and angry with him, he astound at such behaviour. As if all had ill eyes, feelings of driving him out, he felt wherever he went. The bourn, the fields, the bazar's field the idols sanctuary even the sky, they all were fed up with him.

He has understood every one of the village, tasted Cuttack too. He told his mother, at the time of parting that I would go to Bhubaneswar. I would search for any relatives of Baisinga and take rent a house. Then I would take you there.

Having heard this her eyes looked as good as stone eyes of the mask. She usually has no aspiration. Still all her desires remain compact tightly.

After got down from bus, he walked along the bay of the garbage and dirty to reach at a slum. The huts are located very close to each other, as if each holds the hands of other, air can't enter in between in their compactness, no space, everywhere huts. There, he went on searching for relatives of Baisinga. Fortunately, that relative had arranged a rent house at the rate of fifty rupees monthly charge. He can't imagine and it is beyond his prediction and he can't stretch his vision beyond that slum, so vast Bhubaneswar is. They have arranged their own hovel acquiring the Govt. land and the population become high by number. All the tribals from different corner of Odisha have made for themselves a space at Bhubaneswar.

Thus, he to settle himself at certain job, went on wandering now and then from chouk to chouk and in the market of daily labourers. He, rather liked to do his work either under the mansionship of a Telenga, or Adivasi to accommodate him with any varieties of job like wood cutting, concrete cement work, holding lights or watering anything avail to him.

Very competitive is the labour market here. Entire town is busy in construction works, still he can't convince to himself why he is determined for staying in this city after gathering all strength. Yes! A struggle is needed, despite he could hear his own feeble voice. Everything appeared before him disorder, disarrangement. After a deep thought, he decides to ask the relatives of Baisinga for lending him one or two thousands of rupees. He would buy equipments for Masion's job I shall prove others. Still one needs to have basic idea on plan estimation, budget raport with other masions, contractors - no relation, no work.

The relative of Baisinga tried to befool him by reminding that he has arranged all about his stay at Bhubaneswar, now it is my look out to oil my own machine. That relative was doing the job of peon in an office, people of the same slum had opted jobs in different places as per their own choices as well as reached in their achievements. Their thoughts and temperaments were disagreed with their opted life, job and occupation.

Sometimes the slum of daily wagers was bathing in blood by hewing one of the tribals; often the hot film show keep the area warm, most of time the premature infant of a girl was thrown in the bee and lake was seen floating in water; some novels were busy in selling wines and the fronts were engaged in playing cards; some hovels were locked by the obstinate and suspicious husbands bolting their wives inside; some had left for work in factories, some novels were crowded by children, some where children were busy in playing cards game out of excitement.

Still there were untimely excitement of Makar festivals, arranging cock-fighting, drinking handia wine, dancing and many merrymaking items. In spite of all that observations appeared before him weak and farce.

When he was fumbling with narrow mindedness, he had overheard the hearsay about insurgency of going home back.

Again, he sought the help of relative of Baisingh
"I will go back home. Muin Ganke Ferigimi."
Why? Is it for ever? Won't you come back?
'May be?'
You have no likingness for daily wage. Is it possible to get Massion's work easily. If you come I will keep you in my sahib's house by motivating him.

A slave wants to let rest assures to make others slave is the real motif of the entire people of the city. He heard to remember. He guessed the reason of sending him to village, when the bus was approaching towards village from Kaptipada Bus Stand. The woman of the magician was killed by the villagers by misunderstanding her to be witch. Entire villagers were panic striken of police, politics and arrest etc.

Some of them were arrested and others had surrendered themselves to police. Some of our villagers out of fear were wandering in the forest like criminals. The dead body of mother was taken to Baripada hospital for post-mortem. But no one had followed the dead body rather that seemed that as if all were busy in politics.

A group of people came to hug him and console him sounding thundering suggestions and they told that there was pressure from higher level that all would be arrested. Not necessary to be thoughtful, even don't care for anything. In spite of all burden, he tried to become soft like cotton. Where would he search for the dead body of his mother in vast area of Baripada Hospital and that to in midnight. The sweeper, Mehentar may drag the dead body without owner. That sweeper must have thrown the dead body in the jungle area beside the river bed in defecate field. The nocturnal animals must have eaten up some portions of her body.

She usually shivered like Kalis sitting in one of the corner of the room, looked up and moved to middle pillar of the room. What are there in room, only masks made from woods log.

The stone craftsman always gazed at the stone eyed mask. She rose above the level of all demonic, all sorts of fear what have you achieved through out your life? It's only the satire of your male partner. It is the inhuman attitude of the entire village towards your bridship of the Magician's wife. Aren't I mother?

She weeps squeezing tears from her eyes. She had cried like this at the time of birth.

He attempts to match measure the personality of the Goldsmith of Kaptipada with the personality of his not relative of Baisinga living in Bhubaneswar. Soils of both lands equal, not less not more. They throw others diamond and buy the same at the cost of silver. Be it Kaptipada or Bhubaneswar no difference. Equal attitudes everywhere.

Where to return? whether to the company of that fifty rupees rented house beside the drain. Lake of Bhubaneswar where lived half Odia and half tribal people or he would, struggle with himself to be detained on that fifteen decimal patch of land? He stands back to the hut wet in dews and fogs. He kept watching the house to these three wooden masks - and a half made.

He couldn't wait constantly beside the Bus Stop of Kaptipada. He was inconsistence like a new businessman. He was searching something in his bag, they were the only hope of his life.

As if his imaginary plans were talking to him - he was beside the temple of Anugul Chandra. The tribal inhabitants in middle portion. I will install you under that pippal tree. I will construct a temple for your stone eyed wooden mask. I promise mother. I will manage myself out of that income. Rest assure.

INHUMAN

He bound her from top to toe with flocculent in cylindrical way, and crammed green stripped loongi in a poly bag. Then he hauled some cloths around and lifted it on to his head like bole of a banana tree.

Dogs were barking and chasing behind. It was first part of the dark night of Janmastami, Lord Krishna was incarnated in this day. The sound of his crying perhaps had filled pleasure with the heart of the earth. His little daughter was chasing and whimpering after him. It was dawn but without Sun, the elities were just in their morning walk.

They had called upon the residence of the Collector on way to medical. His little daughter spelt out the name 'Jillapala'. There was the vast compound and garden inside; little daughter's emotion became high; she sobbed uncontrollably. Water-cum-mucus dropped from her nose. The SP's residence was in the same row. Almost all were in deep slumber. The watchmen were dozing leaning against the gate.

He did neither have appetite nor thirst nor sleep since last night. He had to carry out that heavy load by shoulder to the remote town with great expectations. As if the road of the town fell stretching long, the unending road was lonely calm and quite. But people suffering from diabetes and obesity were walking sporadic like patients. How could he know? What impression people would have on him viewing such scene along with thirteen years old daughter?

"Yes! They must be thinking that he has certainly cut a tree and carrying that log for selling that in town. Foolish! Nonsense has wrapped a cloth around it. He has come rushing for selling that in cheap rate and will return home after drinking some Mahuli wine."

They were not looking at him. Rather they there had eyes upon the girl in blue dress printed with lyzards painting and walking beside him.

This was first trip to town both for the father and daughter. The pacca roads, people in morning walk, palatial buildings, trees, gardens, long compound walls, parks, playground everything appeared to them new. Their feet in running speed were not delaying for such fascinated things. They didn't have time to keep their eyes in contact with the morning walker to have views of such things in wonder.

A police on duty, blew whistle and had made them stop on the traffic. His stick striked on the cylindrical bundle carrying by shoulder, and asked, "What is in it?" the luggage on shoulder had absorbed and shallowed the striking stroke of the rolling stick. What a wonderful thing! His stick didn't get any respond of stroke? He pulled his loose suit up to waist and looked amazed with suspicion both to father and daughter. Then he had nipped the cloth-wrapped around the cylindrical luggage and scolded to himself for his foolishness - "What a nonsense! Ah! the man got impure early in the morning."

The police man had spattered his hands, turned his head and blown the whistle with instruction, "You leave this place immediately before morning; go back quickly to your village."

He had applied all his strength and sprang like a stick for walking. His daughter stretched like elasticity to chase after him. The sun was just rising his head. The eastern horizon cracked into red colour. After got up from bed a man growing old was spitting elegantly with water and splashed out standing on the yard. Women were shouting and standing in queue with plastic pots and buckets for water in front of a water supply pipe of the municipality. A large number of city crows were cawing and making commotion in Tasmaniar blue gum plant.

The daughter reminded her father, "This road does not run to our village. Reading from a pillar stone. They have left the route in previous chhak." Again, they had both turned back to catch the village road. His eyes were filled with tear, "This is Chandni, his elder daughter, she has gone upto standard five." There is no class after that in the village school." She could have gone to far remote Nakagudi village across river, mountain, forests, lonely place, and many obstacles for higher classes. She did hard labour instead of study. Her little knowledge helped us to recognise the path led to village. Otherwise they would have missed the route and go in wrong direction instead of Melaghara?

In the mean time, he had covered five to six kilometre distance from town to his village via Thuamula-Rampur road. The pungent smell of phenol and the shady of malodour of dustbin of medical was chasing after him. And the patients ward, blood bathing broken iron cot, nurses in white uniform and swelled with discontent and laziness, reporter of blood test, unstruplous doctor who was writing prescription bending his head down, fat-glutton sweeper's high sound vexed word, medical's long yard, and small and big sizes buildings, as if all together of death world's Yamapur were trailing after him. The unknown fear, for heavy loading bundle had made him groaning and feet were trembling uncontrollably but he had not stopped for a moment, the sun-shine was growing tough. The laden of the shoulder was growing heavy weigh slowly.

After sometimes he had to unload the laden. But father and daughter took off that and put that on grass under the Piasala tree and sat relaxed under the tree. They could see the chhak of Sagada village from distance. There was a forest gate ahead. A known person was required to pass us the Gate. In the meantime he had already covered thirteen KM distance from town on foot. The forest begins from Sai Suravi chhak. He would have to go across river, canal, climbed up mountains to reach at Melghara, his village, native place.

Whatever it might be, he had to carry that load to reach at the village before evening at any cost. He despaired looking at the pale and frail face of his daughter and tried to forget his past matters. She couldn't sleep at all previous night.Still there was tears in her eyes, she had still feckless thin sound in her voice. He searched for money in the half folded white shirts pocket and the knot of his two folded green lungi for a five or ten rupee note. But didn't find anything to offer a biscuit to his daughter. All that he had with him being ransacked by the Govt. medical men.

He remembered, how the ticket of two rupees needed to enter into the campus. He didn't have retail money but had ten rupees note. The ticket man answered, "Retail price is not available here - you go, it is adjusted and handed over a ticket to his hand." He hurried to visit the doctor. First that ticket man took his eight rupees note. Doctor had checked and prescribed, for X-ray, blood test and medicine, which were urgent for diagnosis. The Xray operator took Rs. 350/- instantly. The blood test pathologist grabbed two hundred notes. The rest money was spent for saline and medicine. Even a doctor took fifty rupees note for preparing the papers work. All that money he took with him was spent like water dried up in such shine. He became penniless. He remembered himself a water bubble in the empty hand. But that was not bursting, he reached and sat beside the road of Sagada village.

His daughter could read the hungry face of her father. She let out a half drunk water bottle from poly pack and offered her father. He quaffed three to four gulp of draught and gave the rest of it to daughter - "Take and break your hunger with some drops of water." That much water was there for daughter. The dried intestine cracked with new life and energised. He looked at the unloaded laden, the sun shine was dancing on that bundle. Where upon, the hot sun shine was searching for a chink to enter into that to reprimand that. He hurriedly rushed to the laden, bent down to lift that unto his shoulder and moved along the road. A boy of Sagada village stood in front of him and made him stay there, "Wait! Wait, what are you carrying in it? What is that? Tell me, Where had you gone? And where will you go again." "This man may help me a vehicle, as he asks very dearly." He thought in anticipation. He took off that laden from shoulder and put that beside the road. It was intensive hot. He could see the sunshine appeared to him yellow but nothing except that. He knelt and sat in excrete style and talked to that boy very dearly.

"I took her to Nakagandi medical centre, He said", She was suffering from TB and Malaria fever." Disease had been aggravated, and took her to big hospital." I had arranged money and requested my nephew Sitaram for arrange me a vehicle. He did that, "You have brought her in last stage." The doctor said. "What do you think? Give her saline, medicine and stay two or three days in TB ward." "Let's see what happens." He was very caring one among all the patients present in the ward. Patients and their attendants had occupied the beds. I supplicated for a bed to a baboo - he loathed and told, "Nonsense! You sleep on the floor in village but here you demand for bed!" leave this place, you won't be provided a cot." Nothing will be given to you. "I spread cloth on the floor and made her sleep there. She was rolling in ache and blamed to medical and doctors. And said, "why did you bring me here? I would die in my home. It would be my pleasure in company of Sanei and Pramila my two daughters. She went on talking impatiently like a mad man. She told in mid night, "I will die soon, please don't throw me on the street or in any place of the town. You will carry me to village. I will live with other Dumas of my village. Probable it was two or half past two, she passed away. I rushed to nurses and doctors. A nurse had slept bolt the door inside. I knocked at the door and shouted! "Didi… Didi". She got irritated and said, "What happened?" "My wife died" she answered inside. "What should I do?" Carry her to your village."

It was midnight. Daughter was crying. Our crying's sound reached the ward's of the patient. "They're disturbed." Two giant figure men came rushing and instructed us to take the dead body immediately. "Take your dead body. Here patients are sleeping. This is not the place of dead body." They were shouting and repulsed. We both father and daughter lifted her to a darker place of the medical. It was late to be dawn. I requested many baboos for a vehicle to carry the dead body. At last I approached the watch men but they ousted us, "Reach your village before dawn. Otherwise, police will come and demand for post-mortem of the dead body. Investigation will be done. Many complicacies will arise. You can't face them", said the man. All my money was spent in medical. I had no money for vehicle's fair. It would be problem if the dead body was detained there. I thought, "Let me enwrap the body with clothes we had with us. I made it a luggage and carried that to the village Melghara. Baboo, the luggage that you asked about that was the dead body of my Maikina (wife) Amang."

I felt relaxed, as I expressed all these agony at a stretch. Again his daughter cried and whimpered by listening his father's sorrow. The boy had no concern with our matter. Rather he had checked up about the availability of the internet on mobile. This issue would be disappeared in air without proof. Pritam appeared to be happy and had waited till the arrival of the man from town. But he had waited with great anticipation for the help of the vehicle for carrying the dead body. He was calculating that there was forty-eight KMs distance remain to walk after thirteen KM. However, he could not arrange the vehicle at any cost. Again, he was trying to lift the dead body on to his shoulder.

"Wait wait! All the arrangements will be made for you." The boy said. But the time passed. Again he took off that laden from soulder and kept that on the soil. "Silence of the forest was broken by the sound of the bikes, two bike drivers, in black spec carrying heavy bags on their back reached there and asked, "Who is Pritam? Where is he?" They shook hands with Pritam. He showed the case to them and talked to them. Something, what I guessed, they were very happy, talking, laughing was continued. But cremation work was delayed. It was shameful if the dead body would be rotten. Time was passing. He was busy to reach at Melghara. There was no vehicle except these motor bike with two riders. He took an attempt to lift the body on to his shoulder. But a man in black jacket and in black spec came rushing, "listen!

What is asked, you should speak that clearly. You just follow what we speak to you." "We will take your photo.", they prompted.

Again, he kept that the body on the ground at the instruction of the city men. Actually, they were very reluctant in taking the photo snaps. Often city people had come to take photo of their fast and festivals: dance, songs and many cultural programmes. Their photo must be somewhere but they don't get any copy of their photos.

He thought, "Perhaps, these people may take photograph then, will arrange a vehicle later." There was a fat, short height man who was carrying a camera on his back. The camera man was very smart and good looking person - director. He could preserve all the rarest photographs in his camera that thought kept him busy.

The camera man instructed, "Lift that laden on to your shoulder." He did that.

"Move along the road". He just followed the instruction.

"No… no not so fast; walk very slowly feebly." He followed his instruction." The cameraman took the round of the camera upon his daughter. You just make an action of cleanse your face with the handkerchief, walk beside the dead body." She followed. People came rushing and a crowd gathered within few minutes to watch the action of the dead body and daughter walking along with. Chhatrapal, Sabir Mahmmad, Manoranjan Bal, Akrur Bag had already reached on the spot, from town. Again, they were made them seat beside the road after shooting.

He had a trust, that a vehicle would be arranged after that. But there was no end of their cunning decision. The place was echoed by slogans.

Both the competent and aggressive reporters jumped

up. He rang his phone and talked to the man opposite side, "Mam! Good Morning! A dead body is brought from Sadar Sagada Hospital. Wonderful! A man carrying his dead wife on shoulder has come twelve KMs. Is there any news with the administration?" 'Wait' let me inform to an agency, it'll reach the vehicle immediately." "He must be a drunkard tribal man; who has taken the dead body without any permission of the authority. Is this an issue?"

Ok ok, a vehicle is reaching immediately there. The Collector mam was disconnected on phone. A vehicle reached after sometimes. People surrounded the dead body, lifted it to the vehicle and both father and daughter entered into that. The door was locked. People groped their bikes and ran after the city-vehicle inhaling the emissions of the dead body-vehicle

He put the head of the dead body in his lap and legs in the lap of his daughter. He was nodding his head in jolty road and thinking of his three daughters: Chandini, a girl of thirteen years old was walking along with him. He would stay with her some days in Harikana village and had given her marriage in that village; Twelve years old girl, Pramila detained and dropped after class four; Sanei, daughter of ten years was a great for him. Tears run spontaneously when he had a thought about his three daughters and about himself. It couldn't know whether there was anything positive or negative out of nodding in jolty road, the life was like bubble. Driver turned up his head and told, "Vehicle will not move further." After the vehicle crossed Suravi Chhak, Melghara was far away from that chhak. Driver stopped the vehicle and left the seat to open the door of father and daughter, and told, "I can't move the vehicle ahead in this jolty road, could you pay extra money if the vehicle got jalopyed?"

Father and daughter, brought the dead body down co-operating to each other. Again he lifted the dead body of Amang on to his shoulder. The more he moved along up and down the street, more Melghara village was visible. He felt Melghara was the most safest place of the world. No risk all the villagers were like him. The cremation and obsequies should start before the sun set. They had arranged fire wood and called for Disari, it was waited for the arrival of all kith and kins.

He put Amang on the pyre and poured karanja oil. The fire rose from bottom of the pyre, he recollected the company of his wife Sangia, a strange disease entered into her body, nothing could be effective, neither medicine nor doctor nor quack nothing. Sangia died of that disease with severe pain. Charpi was his daughter. He gaveher marriage at the age of nineteen in Singhapur. Both Sangia and Amang passed away. Smoke of the pyre's touched the patches of lands beneath the mountain, that he had prepared them by himself. "Let's stay here not. Lets leave the place."Disari cried. "Thus fire was licking the cracked head of Amang. Again Disari shouted - "leave the place looking to one direction. The shouting of Disari snappished all in one direction. All had washed themselves with turmeric powder then bathed.

All the past tragedy and agony had disappeared in everyday's next day works. All that thoughts of about the exequies 'Dibi' of Amang, would be performed next day. He rushed to Surka maghi, land lord's house. He sat before the landlord in defecate style and cried ululate and did promise to work in his field for incinerated cultivation-shifting cultivation. He had a great expectation upon landlord's co-operation rather, he talked about the Gandhian principle instead of extending helping hand. Right from now you will observe the exequies Dibi ceremony of your Maikina. You must complete the obsequies ceremony at any cost, then you'll touch my land."

When the thoughts of Amang's funeral ceremony expenditure striked to his mind, he looked confounded and strayed. He didn't have his own patch of land. His earnings depended upon the daily wages by working in their fields. He had got this work for fifteen days under NRGS programme of the government, but they took that work back from him. They didn't pay that money instead they told to pay that money later.

He went rushing Singhapur village to bring his daughter Charpee, the elder daughter and left her in the place of moaning. In the same day he went to Horikana village. He delivered the news to the in laws of Chandini. Then he came upon a babbling boy, nephew to him in relation, on way to dear and near one's houses for borrowing money. He was the only boy Dhanda having mobile phone of his own. There is no network here. He had to go to other village, fifteen KMs distance for mobile's network. He stopped his cycle beside them on the way returned from the long distance. He expressed gasped the TV news, that he watched on TV. "Uncle, you have been widely acclaimed, you and Chandni both are playing on the TV screen. Great persons are talking about you."

He stood amazed! what mistake had he done for which the news had been spread outside? What punishment would be rewarded to him. "I had beseeched them a lot while my Amang was alive, she had turned up ashes, why should I request for her to anyone? "I don't understand anything, whatever they like they may do. I have nothing to do." He told his nephew clearly, "I have to perform the Dibi ceremony next morning."

How could he know that? In the mean time the news

had reached in everybody's house through TV and newspaper. That has been viral. He was sleeping with his four daughters, who were fresh like kurei flowers, in Melghara's house. There was no sound, silence was broken by the rattling of the rats, Melghara was in deep slumber and dreamt the fate of her people.

He had dreamt, "Smoke of Dhungia, a ghost, Duma of Amang was sitting in corner of the darkroom. He touched softly with his thin palm to all his four daughters in that dim light."Again that dream disappeared, he got up spooky from that half dream. He predicted, Amang had profound love and affection for her children. Unless she was driven out through 'Dibi', funeral ceremony, her spirit would stay in the room. It needs perfect 'Dibi', to remove that Duma, ghost. Otherwise she would watch the house like witch.

The sun shine appeared energetically in morning, the very day of Dibi ceremony. The wind was blowing sweetly. He came out of hut in deep thought what work should he do first? Three police men arrived in front of his house. One was local but other two were of town area. The same must ache of British realm, fretting and afflicting language, "Both father and daughter get ready, you will have to go to town police station, you have started drama, now get ready a peg for buttock." He spoke spooky, "Today is my Dibi, I have lot of work to do. How could I go?"

"Is your work first or government's order?" Other one had interfered, "keep that Dibi and lanthan next, the Badababu is waiting for you on the midway. You'll have to act according to his advice."

He looked at Chandni with disappointment. He thought, Chandni could assess the gesture what was right or wrong like her mother. Chandni stood leaning against the wall in fear and sorrow like a clay statue. They have come to abduct them. "Be quick, you both father and daughter get ready."

They, both father and daughter got into the vehicle and moved with them in many gradient routes and left Melghara. A red-light vehicle was waiting beside the road. Both the driver and the senior officer sat in front seats. Badababu took off his goggles and found them approaching towards him and scrutinized properly whether they were the same father and daughter to whom he had seen on TV. "Yes! This was the case." You both have to go to town police station. It is the order of the Collector. The BDO sir is waiting for you. They want to talk to you. Our vehicle will bring you to your village again. Now get into the jeep. Hurry up."

He could not understand the intention of the babu whether that was sweet or sour. He had a fear, if they didn't get into the vehicle they might force them to get into. Then they would drag Chandni to go into. This thought compelled him to get into the jeep and told Chandni to follow him.

Amang's Dibi left far behind Melghara. He had accepted himself a water buble, while running with the jeep towards town. The jeep was running to town via Thuamula Rampur. The same route in which he was carrying the dead body of Amang where people were found to be crowded that day. Why he was brought to town on the very day of Dibi, he couldn't understand that and what punishment he would be awarded for nothing. Both father and daughter felt themselves like soft-velvet puppet in their hands. "What do they predict?"

In the town, the flags of different political parties were fluttering there for him. Medias were shouting political TRPC for him. TV reporters holding booms in front of the Magistrate and buzzing around her by asking questions, "Madam! What is your view on this matter, being the head of the administration?" Magistrate mam was non Odia, so his pronunciation was very peculiar with fragmentary Odia. She wore a powerful glass. Magistrate said, "That man took the dead body without information of anyone." What was the fault of the administration?" Drops of saliva was falling from his long tongue to and fro." How could she know this?

There the time of Dibi ceremony was delaying. All the near and dears of his clan must be waiting for him without bathing and eating and blaming to Amang. However, many police were watching to both father and daughter. The BDO sir was not present there. They would be allowed to go to village after arrival of the BDO. Every moment appeared to him an eon. After a long time the Saheb's vehicle arrived. He matched the figures on TV with the appearance of father and daughter and entered into his cabin by nodding his head. Both of them, were sent for a meeting inside the chamber after waiting for a long times. The door was bolt inside. The office was carpeted, clean attractive chairs and table and vase were arranged, both father and daughter stood huddle in the corner of the AC room. The BDO blamed them collecting words from air, 'Then you have murdered your wife and carried to village. Am I right?"

"No Sir! I have not killed her, she died by herself." The BDO sir told in stuttered voice, "Take these five thousand rupees for expenditure. If anyone asks you, you should tell them, you have taken the dead body from medical without informing to anyone." He told boldly at the time of parting, "Stop your mouth about this matter. Otherwise you will be accused of murder to your wife and imprisoned."

He was not shocked at this statement rather the feeling of hatredness sensitised him. "The truth I have come upon and experienced very painfully, they have turned up false and warned him to hold his tongue not to express anything before anybody." He didn't have any idea if anyone could stop his mouth at the threat of some body's false accusation.

On the way to catching the red light vehicle from BDO sir's office. But his mouth opened spontaneously. The media men surrounded with to competition among them and shovering with each other to take a bite. They asked, "what did the BDO sir tell?"

"I do not know how to tell lie. He told me,"turn up the truth upside down to lie, and gave me five thousand rupees."

The red light-vehicle left him two miles away from Melghara. He ran towards village for Dibi before setting of the sun. The ceremony of Dibi started after they arrived.

'Dhartani', the Earth is underneath and the sky overhead; A big firework was performed in the company of the kith and kin. 'Mahuli', the wine poured into fire Dumbin Dumbin pot filled. The five tribe men drank Mahuli, then they ate rice and Kandul dal. All were congregated to song the lament song, thereafter they had danced the traditional tribal dance with the song written in blood. Melghara nestled peacefully.

If a village lying sleep peacefully, one must not disturb her. This was not new for Melghara but the most value based principle of Melghara. Melghara was becoming crowded by the bustle of outsiders.

He sat on his yard with his daughters Chandni and Pramila. A man in gorgeous white dress sat on mud floor and picked up Sanei to his Lap and took the pose in front of camera. People shouted with flag and slogan, jindabad behind the man.

The people who had reached at his village way faring

sixty kms distance from town and the people of Khandadhar village joined the procession by group wise giving slogan 'jindabad, murdabad. Melghara echoed by their sounds. One of them took Sanei to his lap and said, "You'll say what is asked to you and take some money."

Two babus came rushing early in the morning with much worriness and tapped his door and got me up, handed a big bundle of note to me and had assured me to register my name to get many things, if he would stop declaring anything. They advised me, "You may oil your own machine. Take care."

They had come early in the morning in fear of camera. The delaying caused of gathering media, CBI, social activists and stired Melghara. Only interviews of his tragic incident was going on. "Did he know all this?" Radio was sounding, photo snapping so and so were like hot cake. He had put on a Tarla, (cap made of leaves) on his head and moved around the place of ceremony.

His news had spread all over the world, his photo, his reaction, his problems in newspaper, YouTube, TV, Radio, Facebook, Twitter and about the message of condolence of Prime Minister and with so many. Poems, stories, cartoon etc. all were shouting a lot about him. So many things were going on. But he was busy in weeding of Parighasa and spading the cultivated land of his master.

Even if there was no rest in that working place. People of media in jeans, scotes, shoe, phono, colour goggles were climbing the mountain and to reaching at him. He was about to bend work in the field, again he had to stand straight in front of boom. Now he opened his mouth half, "My maikina died, my children became orphan but those baboos are coming and ask me same questions time and again and displeased me. Could you not let me live happily? You should let me live peacefully with our problems. Don't make us bother."

He had accepted himself a water bable in the thought to these activities who had forgotten his own name. Whereas the entire world had remembered his name. He became acclaimed all over the world for sympathy, news, politics, conflict etc. The very term 'Dana'. The gift he remembered his own name then added his title Majhi after that name. Khalifa of Baharin sent Rs. 9,00,000/- by his name. His nephew came rushing with a news, he had seen on TV. He amazed at the news of becoming man of lakhs?" "What does mean by man of lakhs. He didn't know how could run a business with that money? He did not know the technique of becoming zamindar with that money. He had acclimatised himself with the income of his daily wages. He did not know what to do with the surplus money of his daily wages.

It was unknown to him how media failed to draw the attention of the people for him. He became rancid in the world of the news. Viewers were interested for fresh sensitive news. All channels and news papers highlighted the photo of dead body on the shoulder of Dana Majhi being followed by some near and dears crying in anticipation of some money from people. Sometimes people were carrying patients on cot, somewhere some dead bodies, a kind of drama were displayed on TV screen. Media was playing them with new issues, as if they were managing viewers with new type of issues. Panchayat election was ensuing. Then media was diverting attention towards that. One day his nephews came with news, "You're neither on TV nor in newspaper. Now you are nowhere."

"I'm here! at Melghara", he answered with variety. He didn't have time to think about the world outside. Pari grass was growing in the field. These piriweed was enemy of the growing crops. He was weeding out that piri grass. The water drops of the sweat were being coloured by the sunshine.

He was sent for from field to village. One out of two baboos told, "You'll go to Delhi." He amazed at the new problem came upon him. He showed some papers and said, "Khalifa's messenger will give you a cheque for Rs. 9 lakhs in a meeting. It is our look out to take you for Delhi and again bring you back to your village after the work is over."

He put on clean cloth and got into their vehicle, then broaded to Delhi from Bhubaneswar. He was taken to big hotel, food, decoration, gorgeous living made him think, living in a fairy world, he added Amang in his tear-wet eyes, "It is only for you! Amang. This capital Delhi, broaded in aeroplane and life has become full of charitable life.

A meeting was organised in Delhi for him. Among the VIPs the meeting was held and handed over a cheque for nine lakhs rupees. "What would he do with money after deposited in his account."

He was taught like parrot by people in Delhi meeting. If anybody ask you then say, "I will spend that money for the education of my three daughters." A man translated that into English and declared the statement English. Nay there started clapping.

He only, remembered Melghara. He dreamt a wonderful dream : A light was burning with flame in a lonely and foggy night, Hundreds of new and old Duma, phantoms of Melghara sat around the piles of notes. Keeping them middle. His first wife Sangia was also present too along with Amang. Black foam of new with cohered at her mouth. The poison of hatredness was brimming on the green eye ball of yellow sclera of eyes. Exactly Amang rose from the group of Dumas and kicked at the piles of notes. "Our lives are not that cheap like money." All the Dumas of Melghara laughed screaming at the statement of Amang. They all disappeared squeaking from his dream.

The red catwalk runs to Melghara and repaired by the contractor had been washed by heavy downpour, I saw on the way back to village from Delhi. A word slipped of tongue, "What shall I do with this big amount of money?" That is true in all point of view. That money will be deposited in his account. A fund will be created by his name. A trusty will be formed. Then he will turn up a bee hive for others. All the people, dear and nears from village and clan will come to him to flattering, the touts social worker, political lieutenants, followers, will make crowd around him like bug, worm, insects to eat his flesh and blood. How could he know who is who?

Again, Melghara had grown back to her own ancient form. Alasi flowers were blooming from buds. There was no overcrowd of camera men, reporters, social activities, white dressed elites of outside and slogans of petty political people, nothing. Except the rare visits of chowkidar, forest guards in Kaman. There was no overcrowd of reputed persons. Now he is happy with drinking of jurum, eating of mandia gruel and feeling warm sleeping with his three orphan daughters. Again, he would climb up mountains and come down in evening, how could he know that he has been arrested in red file of outside world. One day there was a long argument on him in between the ruling party and opposition leaders but that became calm and cool down after sometimes.

One day he remembered how was he becoming a water bubble after death of Amang. He would about to burst out at any moment. But had not seen! How the inhumans are effeminate. They are so incompetent to let a blister burst. Then, he smiled at this attitude of the effeminates.

LISTEN O GOVT. LISTEN

Better not to ask about the governance of Gurudipanka. Here administration means, it is wish of the village watchman. He makes all illegals legal and demonstrates his power.

Why the village road became muddy? Deposit two hundred rupees. Why do you both brothers quarrel intoxication, Deposit fifty rupees.

Forest guard comes and behaves like next to government. Otherwise I will arrest you.

Have you pet oxen-poda. They all destroy our forest. Deposit rupees one for each cow and podha-oxen and fifty paisa for each goat or get yourself ready for arrest.

All the three governments usually spend their time in ward member's residence pleasurely. They are : Kumuti's government, Mahajana, money lender government and half-politicians, Kujineta. They eat drink and share among them self the boiled chicken, Mahuli wine in the residence of ward member.

The ward member is not less than a government too.

Give money. I will give you old age pension. Give money for buying of papers and stamping to enlist in BPL record. Money is demanded for each work.

Our children take birth amidst many governments. I

have been listening many fairy tales since childhood : the story about different governments, Sarkar. I observe the varieties of opinion of government like different winter garments.

They shout. They threaten - they exploit - they arrest. All the doors and windows of the village are shut down at the arrival of Govt. The Sarakar, governments order to close the schools. They instruct the magistrate to share fifty percent of his salary. Go and sit home.

No need of construction of roads. Give something to us - take bills - the Sarkars dissuade the contractor.

You just dig polls, they direct to the electrician to sell the wires and equipment and give our share.

Here, no need of either of doctor, or pharmacist or nurse, we depend upon witchcraft. You share your salary with us and go home and enjoy your time. Treat the patients with private fees.

If tubewell is dug no matter. Get arranged for some drops of drinking water.

Nobody can't cook country wine. Licences were provided to Sundhi, Kumuty. You all go and buy that and drink. Excise government frighten us and leave the place away.

Dasu has been observing these governments since his childhood. The more governments are the more ethics and modality. Dasu surprise at the number of governments. It is not only the conflicts among the govenments. They also merry make among themselves. They share everything among themselves pleasurely. You stay frighten - not necessary to know either about the government or about the world outside. You remain like that unchanged. Live like animals, die like pigs and be Duma. Phantom after death. Dasu can study the Mindset of the government. He runs to neighbour village to get himself educated next side of the mountain. However he passed standard seven. He fights for education, and obstinate for learning. His father was destroyed for this wine. Mother is suffering from certain disease. His family suffers from poverty. There are dogmas, foolishness, discourtesy, savaging in every and each home of Gurudipanka. It is only fearness spread like anything. Dasu becomes disturbed and uptight for the sorts of problems both in family and village. He climbs the Danger-Hill and sit at the end partitioned on a stone. Both the pain of the villagers and pain of his own becomes own unitedly. He dipped in emotion, composes poems for these villagers, for his Qui Community and Sora-Kandha people. He has friends in his villages. He unite all the boys and girls, 'Dhanda Dhandis' and form as party. They move to marriage ceremony, festival and fast and parting of brides. They dance and sing there-Dasu can compose songs as well sings. His voice is very enchanting. The thrilling voice of Dasu revibrate with dance, song and entire forest echoed by it.

Dasu observe, Kui people become less interested for dance song by and by. He never finds fult with others but his own Kui men. Actually, they are mostly responsible for such downfall who have been baptised by giving a dip in water. They are taught and motivated not to practise that Qui song and dance and cock sacrifices which are not permissible in Christian religion. Jesus Christ may get angry if you do this. Qui people are wearing sacred thread like Hindus. They bring Hindu cassettes and play that in village and dance in tune of that music.

Dasu finds himself intolerable to such type of attitudes of the youngsters. Dasu pursue, and convince to the people from village to village not to give up our own culture, own song, whatever custom they may accept. This is our source religion. It's only the landlords and govt. both divide us and categorise us for votes, nothing else. Dasu observe the soot, the savaged things in his own village. He, along with his party, set out his journey to eradicate the superstitious things. Tigers eat to poors and rich both. Why the necromance comes to the poors not to riches. Is the God choosy? They have planned to entangle that superstious thing with the poors. They have applied that necromancy, magic conservative things and to create violence among us. If you suffer from fever, take quinine medicine. Don't go for magician and sacrifice cocks.

Dasu compose songs on this affairs. He tries to change the mind-set of the people by singing the song. People are addicted of alchohol of his own village, this attitude makes him intolerable. This wine may destroy their lives, what happened to his father. People pledge themselves in the house of the landlords. On the otherhand the business of sundi, money lender, wine shops are increasing in lips and bound. The whinning sound of dead person's near and dear are heard. It is the feeling of lamentation is heard yammering everywhere. Dasu's heart awaken at the pain and strain of his community. He starts composing songs against wine. This traditional songs when they are recited, the people of his community become emotional by these magical and melodious playing.

As per tradition, Dasu, feels it important to pay 'Kenda', cows, oxen, brass utensils as dowry to the brides, Dhandi by the Dhandis. For which the grooms, Dhanda mortgage their lands and utensils.

Being one of the leading men of the communities, Dasu educate people to eradicate these dowry systems and let the groom pay some amount of money to the brides. Again, Dasu feels, this is also a problematic thing. It may be difficult for Dhanda, the groom for arranging such amount of money. Again Sabukar, the money lender become rich more and more. Both the Dhanda and Dhandi remain starve after marriage.

Dasu, having modern outlook, tries to make them understand for love marriage or develop affairs before marriage and don't give any dowry to anyone.

Dasu, composed songs with the theme of these thoughts. There was certain magical power in writings of Dasu, but people applied their second thought to interpret the meaning of the songs what Dasu says, are they true or false? Whether they are right and good to us? Dasu's idea injected in the blood of youngs. They had adopted affair marriages by and by. The marriage went on in this process.

Now Dasu finds his compositions obsolete and off key about marriage songs. When a book of marriage ceremony's song of 'Kuidin punga' reached his hand. Dasu had to change the theme of his songs after long observation of the condition of the people and Govt.

The day Dasu changed the pattern of dress of leaves. Colour loongi folded by inned banian inside it and drew the tambour on to his breast for bangging, the singers of his party followed him.

This region of kui, its language
Oh, dear let us unite for it.

Dasu made himself ready for the prosperity of Kui people with dedication. He wanted to take all sorts of initiative for his community.

His songs impact created an off season of business for wine shopkeepers. His songs made people cleverer than before, people responded the forest guards properly without fear of them. Dasu's song stopped the exploitation of homeguards. Giving subscriptions to Sarakars were stopped.

His song made dance the government. Then government lodged a complaint against the song in the police station of Mandimera.

The officer of the Mandimera police station had sent for Dasu and introgated him.

"Stop writing songs"

Today, right now, you may stop of composing songs. Dasu thinks, Govt. speaks today to stop composing of songs. Tomorrow will demand to stop talking. Next day may demand you quit the village. I, just can't do it. He had been observing the glaring of these people since his childhood. He will never scare of their red eyes. He composes song and people have proper respond of it and reformed them. Has he carried rifle, Govt. scare of him.

Do the Govt. have fear of song? He innocently asks this questions to himself, he chortle.

In front of his eyes, he observes, how the police and Government ransack his village, Gurudipanka. They come, time and again, in the heart of hot, midday or in silence of darkness, midnight, blow the whistle and plunder the village.

You have hidden the rebellions and agitators in village you keep them close to you.

The quietude of the village broke in their sounds. They intrude the village by the names of agitators and behaving like plunder one, the police grabbed the ration card and twelve hundred rupees from the hand of Khauti Majhi. Other day, in continuous process, the police carried out capsicum, gramblack, kandula dal and many edible things from his home. The same thing happened with Kasu Malik and Sultan. Police broke the lock of Prakash and entered into his home, found nothing but fifteen rupees from a tin canister. Police didn't find anything from Macla Majhi's house but ate up cooked beef from the earthen pot and finished everything.

In every sudden attack of the Govt. on Gurdipanka, the rate of pulsating of heart breathing becomes high. He shapes his cry, his hatredness, his stimulation in literature. His triumphant hatred fiery cascade song against government, people got by heart that and exalted. Audience demand this Bedanda song of Dasu, if that is an occasion of Kui or Soura people gathered to listen Dasu. In his hot breathing, adds fuel like jute stick by playing of tambour and the tuning becomes high. Spontaneously, the hands of people armed with arrow and bow, axe, flute, stick raised up at the tuning of the song.

Dasu compose songs with eyes

Kui people looked with wide eyes

The administration and Government close their eyes.

Dasu's pursuation, only for the wellbeing of his men, thus, the word of his songs shoot like arrow, Dasu walks on fire, jumping and jumping.

Listen o' Listen. It is heard, Dasu is absucunded. His music party, all astound at this news, the villages nearby Gurudipanka could not take in granted. The worn out, spetugenerjan mother's eyes were running with nonstop tears, wife became bed ridden, having heard of this news. Everywhere, at the place of cultivation at Bena Munda where meetings of the clan was going on be it at bathing stream or in bazar, a single talk - Dasu is obscured.

Whispering went on that God ate up Dasu.

Some opined, "Dasu has gone either to Delhi or to Mumbai for more reputation.

Listen! News has come, two Andra greyhound police riding on bike in civil dress Dasu picked up in railway station and took him to police station. This news, in one side, there was merrymaking, and people exult with triumph of the Govt. in Gurudipanka. Dasu is absent, Sundhi Govt. (sarakar) have come to kick his belly. The government reaped the riped corns cultivated by Dasu.

Again, they began plundering and feign of the governments in search of rebellions. The same type of loot took a new shape. It is better to say, the terrorism of the terrorist govt.

Dasu, behind a cabin, just at the chauk of station was pissing, two greyhound police picked up Dasu. Dasu was crying, "What is my fault? where are you carrying me? Report me before the police of Odisha, let the Govt. decide my fault."

They became deaf at the approach of Dasu. Rather they had asked for letter. No letter was with him. He was not carrying message to anyone. Dasu replied, "I didn't have any letter with me, I have the script of my composition."

They, let Dasu held a lively bomb - "You just carry this and declare yourself naxal."

I'm not Naxal. Why should I carry this bomb. I am a poet, I am man of pen."

They never hear any request of their hunt.

They don't understand the language of the prey

They undressed him and pushed him into the dark lock up.

Next day, they tied his legs and hands and forwarded him from Kamarda police station to Parvatipuram police station. Bijay Kumar was the police office in that police station, appeared like tiger, appropriate to his appearance. Beat Dasu hard, Dasu fell half dead. They took four hundred rupees from his pocket. P. Vijay Kumar, found a wrist watch from his pocket for his own pocket.

They felf Dasu, a lively danger for them. They don't let Dasu stay in one place. They sent him to a conceal place of Vijaynagar under the custody of Vijaynagar police Dasu felt a little relaxed viewing the presence of Odisha police. Because they will understand his language. They may understand and his request. They may take him from the encountering greyhound police custody to their custody. He looked at them with great expectations.

They, the Andra police put the bionet of the rifle in Dasu's mouth. Odisha police asked Dasu, "Tell, if you know about the Naxal or put on the Naxal dress and let us move to Odisha."

One thing Dasu was repeatedly saying, "I am a poet as well as a singer too."

All these things happened in response of your song. In presence of the Andra police, Odisha police had begun its interrogation and beating hard. How could Andra police remain silence spectacular, they joined in beating work with robber pipe. That pipe broke into pieces. He was rolling on the ground like a ball - the Kui poet. There was an old Odia police he told, "No sympathy for this man. Let him sleep on the rail line."

Andra Police pulled him out from the ground. They let him hold a slate. "I'm Jayaram Majhi, Naxalite." written on it.

Dasu blinked his cracked eye lid and saw, they have made him duplicate Jairam Majhi and took his photograph. He retaliated in his cracked lips, "I am not Jayram Majhi, I am Dasuram Maleka."

They became unkind, did not listen his request. They succeeded by arranging false witness against him and reported him in Babuli court. The court sent him to the jail of Visakhapatnam. After some days, Odisha police arranged false case matter against him and brought him to Odisha jail, then to R-Udaygiri prison. Again, he was transferred to

Paralakhemundi jail. Dasu had to spend one year and four months time in different jails like a bad dream.

The day he was realised from jail and his feet had touched the soil of his village Gurudipanka, he looked different after severe pain and strain. Still, the cicatrice of previous punishment of the police were not healed. But a glimpse of a ray of happiness about his release from jail was gleaming on his eyes.

He was not given a chance to meet his mother and wife, the Govt. had discarded his request. This sixteen months time had made his family deserted, they looked different. Govt. had harvested the crops of a year income from his field. His lands were scattered in plundering. Dasu, when he raised his head from oppression, the appearance, the scene of that devastation sprang before him. Both the pasture land and his cultivation field appeared to him alike.

Dasu had come back, after sixteen months all the old and youngs Dokra Dokris, Dhanda Dhandis surrounded him like Kurei flower.

They feel better in presence of Dasu

They appreciate his compositions

They like the tune of Dasu, if he sings

They, find them pleasant in company of Dasu.

As if, after a decade, what their attitudes reflected. They have not heard the enchantingly songs of Dasu. The song of Dasu, as if, since long, have not instructed the Kuis, what they should do what not.

A child of his village asked, "You must have composed a lot of songs in the prison."

It is only my song, what promoted them to put me in the jail. 'jail', the significance for me and I was criminal in that place for them. Why they would give me pen and papers for writing? Rather the hearth and the charcoals in it, became pen and paper for my compositions. Yes, I could not compose songs inside the jails but I have made letter and alphabets, for Kui community. Once, a jailor of R-Udaygiri jail, smiled crookedly Ah! You compose poems? People, the party of Collector of information from Bhubaneswar are asking about you. News are published in your name. What type of poet you are? What sorts of poem do you write? Whether you are the poet of Kui, Odia or Telegu language? I replied to him, "I write in Odia script in Kui language." He asked enthusiastically, "Don't you have scripts for Kui language?" I answered, "No". he suggested, "Hy - you make scripts for your community, let them learn and read, let them accept that Kui letters and language. Since then, I have tried to make Kui alphabets. Writing with charcoal on the jail floor and succeeded by completing this within six months.

Dasu darted his hand into pocket and brought out a piece of paper four folded. Opened that before his neighbours. They saw that letters with wide eyes. The alphabets were appearing like attractive paintings, Dasu had prepared alphabets for his Kui men for the first time.

We have got alphabets

Dasu, is the only inventor - saviour.

We will learn alphabets - we write it.

In the crowd of happiness, Dasu was standing at the centre like an inventor. One of the Dhanda, young men held by the waist of a Dhandi, girl to dance in the tuning of the Dasu's song, someone let Dasu hold a lambour to play with changu, songs over flows from Dasu spontaneously.

In this region of Kui community

Our Kui language came up

Let us write to save this

Make strong bondage and unity

To rise with great hope.

In dance and merrymaking for the emotions of the song, courage of the song and their demand of the song, the rejoice of darkness flow to midnight. In the meantime, a thought of publishing a alphabet books in Odia and English language striked to mind. Children of Kui community will get this pleasure privilege to build their future. They will learn alphabets with picture. Day may come, all will write in Kui language.

Villages, adjacent to Gurudipanka and hamlets of near by forests, all people of Kui, Soura and Kandha men of all communities have special affection and regards for Dasu. The oppression of the Govt. became dim before that love. Dasu applied ointment in his wound.

Again, he started writing

Again, returned to the world of creativity

Set right all his devasted land.

Play volleyballs with the junior boys

In village, Dasu shared all his evening times with the village children and let them learn Kui language moving from door to door.

Dasu excited. Dasu feels that everything is going on well but the forest, mountain, fountain, all these perhaps, there was certain disorderness Dasu could sense that. Four months duration during summer the land become deserted. Water flows in brook unused whereas the lands remain dry. Govt. had eaten all money that was scrutinised for digging of canal.

Intensive hot overhead. Hunger in stomach, no food with anyone, nothing to give assurance to money lender. Mango stone were piled in one of the corners of the room. In hard time, it is only gruel and mango stone dependable. People become very worried and feeble by eating all these inedible food stuffs and they become weak and malnutriate due to lack of appropriate food. All the tube wells of all villages are become out of order in rainy season. People have no alternative to drink but water of the bourn and stream. There was neither medicine for dysentery, nor medicine for fever nor availability of doctor. During rainy season people died of cholera and malaria like anything.

They are ignorant, savage, they understand nothing, they eat stale-rotten beef, they eat fungus, mango stone and drink stale gruel. They eat wild poisonous fruits and drink bourn's water. Say, these are usual common food item for them at the time of scarcity.

That, government remain silent, think about them but Dasu brood over the matter. He becomes serious for his men. The rain of sympathy and compassion flows in his heart.

If, there is sound of cry and whinning from a distance village blows from, Dasu aware of the break out of epidemic.

No time for Dasu to compose songs during this needful time. Villages suffer severely and writhe from diahorria and malaria. Dasu's works remain overburdened. Dasu accompanied by his music party moving by from door to door and educate them to drink boiled water, keep clean the surrounding to be conscious of heath and Dasu made himself busy providing service to the bedridden septugenerian, if they are suffering from any disease. He cleans stools in their homes, care of the distress and destitute. He send for medicine to Gallimara village for the sufferers. So that lives of the people could be saved. If there is not a quack in Gallimora village, therefore, the man returns to village without medicine.

Dasu, always present with the suffered. Make himself engaged, washing their slots and pour drop of water in their mouths, consol him moving his hands at back and wait for medicine from Gallimora village. Joseph again will get up smart. But before him, the life of Joseph passed away.

Dasu returned to Gurudipanka, getting news of outbreak of epidemic there. Joseph was one of the members of his music party. All his tears dried up - why should he weep for a single man. Entire village was bed ridden in cholera. Dasu finds no alternative no substitute, situation had made him mad. He was moving here are there to save their lives. He was fighting with two hands against cholera. Dasu had no time to think about himself, the thought of food deleted from his memory. His sleeping became disturbed and disordered.

Man, who was running for day and night, Dasu himself was contaminated by this. First he felt stomach ache, then nausea and fever and water like stool streamed from his annus.

Hue and cry spread everywhere, Dasu in suffering from Cholera. All came rushing to see Dasu. All had cried for his suffering.

No, anyhow, we have to save this poet, singer, musician man at any cost. The pied piper, the man of hearts of young and old, should have to save. The man who encouraged us to fight against govt. we have to fight with death for his life.

Dasu was trying to convince them that there was no chance of recovery in nicromacy but medicine. The young men and women, Docra and Docri and Dhangda and Dhangdi are dieing in large degree without medicine. Where to get medicine, one of them had a knowledge that the doctor team are working in Birikot village, seventeen KM distance from Gurudipanka. Two Dhangdas set out their journey to Birikot to bring medicine for Dasu. Dasu will recover if he takes medicine. Again, he will write poems. He will teach

Kuwi letters to Kuwi children. Again, his song will encourage the villagers to live like a human being. With the thought for recovery of Dasu, that two Dhangdas, went rushing seventeen kms distance the Birikot village.

All people of Gurudipanka sat in prayer for Dasu's get over. They were waiting for the medicine too. Temporary medicine camp was running in Birikot. The hue and cry of the media, the city doctors were bound to come with a camp. There was a crowd of the people there. Medicine stripes were piled beside their hands. Some of them had come over rocky lane and fane, across the hills, twenty-five kilometres and some were shivering in fever and came with hardship of walking. Patients were everywhere in everybody's home. Epidemic in village and patients at home. Almost all were busy for taking medicine for their people. All were desirous, hundreds of skeleton hands were stretched towards the doctor and nurses.

Two Dhangdas of Gurudipanka had come back with medicine. They trotted seventeen kms distance to Gurudipanka. What happened to Dasu? Was he waiting for medicine? They ran trotting, their excitement was overflowing.

O Govt.! It won't be good for you. If Dasu will die. Anger enraged their pulsation, there was an echo of cry in forest.

At last they reached at the neck of the village. They were carrying medicine in their hands. The medicine packet dropped from their hands. Dasu was no more to eat that Govts. Medicine.

MANGO STONE

After a long times, a torch procession irradiating the forest set out from our village. We, all were whimping holding the torch.

The journey of our torch procession was stopped in midway. 'Mandu', newly cooked rice was put in the cleft, earthen pot as per the rytheme of our system. We all moved towards cemetery under the borax discarding them by legs. We had put the fire wood systematically. We kept on the the dead bodies of Marsha Majhi, Chandra, Gahadi, Kumuti, Lachhi, Sarojini, Wana, one by one. We poured caster oil on their heads and set fire, kindled in them. Disari was with us. He shouted and warned us to leave the place immediately cul-de-sac. Damba, and Barika followed his saying : "Leave, leave at once."

They were transformed 'Duma' phantom frizzled on fire in seven wooden piles. They must have been disappeared in air and mixed in the starry sky of our village of mountain regions. We returned home after bathing in Bourn.

The moon was peeping out behind the Kodingmala hill. Darkness had spread her wings through criss-cross space of the distance and near mountains surrounded by Fog and Mist. We had returned to village in dim light but wimping of our 'Maiji', women and 'Dhangdi', Maids had not been ceased till that time of lonely night.

Our working hands in the crop fields were very slow and almost stopped in progress. Our minds were neither in wine nor gruel. We would think of other matters after nine day's exorcise of funeral ceremony.

A talkative man, 'Kuhalia', had reached in that day and searched for Vijaya, "is there Vijaya-Vijaya?)". "I'm Vijaya." Vijaya stood there and Budhabudhi, old man and women, Dokra-Dokri, both male and female youths Dhangda Dhangdi of Panasaguda village all stood beside him. He came horridly breathless on cycle to Panasguda village. First he had smoked Dhungia, (dry leaves of certain tree that makes the smoker inebriate) First he made wet his throat and said, "Your village is published in newspaper, wait what will happen?"

He had come from Kasipur to Panasgunda to tell this much news. He smoked our Dhungia and drank Tumbie salap in Nautumba. The messenger delivered the message. We usually remain busy in nine days, Spectre ceremony of Dumbi, and birth and days activities of our clan. We didn't have time at all to know about outside world. We were least concern about them.

A big fire was flared in middle of the village Dumbi filled pots to salap wine were poured into it. Black cocks necks were controt for each Duma, fire combustioned drinking the blood of black cocks-Duma drank them. The priest chanted unclear Garud Marud hymns. Thereafter, Mahuli wine was given away among our tribe and clans. We never mix water in Mahuli to adultrate it which would have direct impact on rainfall. Unknown fear would come up untimely. Mahuli wine boiled our blood we revealed for a night. Those who were ours own last day they, all turned up Duma today, let them live peacefully as Duma.

We have not completed our nine days spectre ceremony yet, A news reached in us that Suruda Majhi, Salem, Sada, Piala Majhi and other four people of Bilamala village had breathed their last and turned up Duma. A cry of whimping sound was vending through the crevasse of the mountains by breaking the dark silence of night - A cry - ho hulla of death's panic was running high.

A man shouted, "Is Vijaya there?" Vijaya came and stood in front. The number of note-pads, pens and camera were moved in number than the people had come. They all had moved to every nook and corner of the village. The madams in jeans dress were merrymaking with our Dhangdis and maijies. Some of them were taking photos to make them seat near mango stone piles, beside the mango stone flour and at the pose of drinking of Jurum-wine. Once the camera-party had come during puspuni-ceremony and took the photograph of our dance and song. We always dance like dolls in front of camera lenses. That was the time of observation and mahuli session. We the Dhanda and Dhandi were dancing arm in arm.

But now the moaning of death has deplored the atmosphere. Those who died last day, they remained with us in form of Duma and observe all our activities. Could these camera take photograph of these sacred Dumas? They left the place merrily in vehicles after photo session. A day was dallied unnecessarily for that photo session.

Rain bore down over Kodingmala hills, the wild rain was invading by making fearful sound. The deluge was pouring down in gust. The rain abated making jhumpur-jhain sound but inclemency. Here rain has may types of rhythms and dances. Somebody were garreting fuel woods and others were making Tarla-Tarli rain coats with piasala leaves for rain. The oil of kusum flowers were prepared grinding that oil is very useful for massaging in rain-wet body to get oneself warm. The rain opened the tragic death about the memories of the buried past. The spasmodic thoughts of the dead people were blossoming the details of tragic memory of our hearts, by drizzling. Right the time someone had called, 'Where is Vijaya?'

Vijaya came and stood infront. The Dhanda, Dhandi, Damba Disari Barika stood surrounded of the talkative-kuhalia. He sat down beneath the dried salap tree and smoked Dhungia.

"The news of the village has been spread all over the world. The supreme court condemned the state government for misuse of rice-give them to rats instead of people." Delhi parliament was vibrating at the shouting of oppositions. Centre slipped and shifted the responsibility to state saying. "The store room is full of food what should we do, we have no falt with us if the state will not take care what should centre do?" Govt. Here declared that, people were dying eating poisonous food. A senior officer told, "these are the proterious food." There was no matching among the opposition leaders. Your problem had become a hot discuss outside.

We don't have time to watch that drama. People those who have no landed property, he would go for 'Kulubhuti', daily wages carrying gruel and with them to the field. That was time for making embankment, tilling lands, sowing seeds, preparing mud and covering all that works we had prepared the patches of land beneath the mountain, spading them in summer for sowing 'Suan', 'Alasi', 'Mandia' and 'kandula dal'. They were foliating in first touch of rain water. Pari grass were growing big amidst them. We have to weed out them from field through Kudkakudiki.

We feel very hungry during this time. We usually

didn't have any food at home. Danger has been deforested wilde Arum, leek are not available in those time sometimes our children returned from hunting with rats, Rat snake, bird's egg, tree ant, fly ant. Sometimes it is our hunger seethe with great pleasure at the taste of strong fried of fly ants. During the time of 'Kumari' for hunger - searched for Vijaya.

"Where is Vijaya?"

Vijaya came up and stood before them.

They, three people had come. One was Hedu of the Laxmipur police station. The Garudu (guard) of forest. The last one was RI. They were all our Administrators. They called to Kandha, Paraja, Jhadia, Saunta, Damba, Barika, Disari, Bejuni, all professionals for tribal traditional observations. We all remain present before them. The three governments stood in rain coat in heavy down pour, Jhapur Jhain rain on village street. Some of us were with them wearing 'Tarla tarli', (cap made from leaves for rain) and umbrella, Chhatachhati to atain their calls. All the Dhandi (women) middle age women, Maiki spinsters, Dokradokri and old men and women were observing the situations with wonder standing on veranda of the narrow rows of the huts.

The RI sir, out of the three sarakars made us conscious with strict order, "The news of your village has been turned serious. Keep your eyes open. Ministers, MLAs, senior officers may come to your village. Be ginger. Be aware the chief, Hedu was gaoling to rain with his stick, glaring eyes. Uttering slang, gyalpa, "you'll drink musty gruel without washing out the earthen pot. You'll eat poisonous mushroom cooked it relish and let others eat him to kill. You'll give snaps to camera. Okay, Right now, get yourself ready."

The three sarkar got into the vehicle. We, all shut our door and went for sleeping.

The deserted cry of Biswanath Majhi was heard in

lonely midnight of the village. His mother was died. His wife died too he had lost his two and half years son too. Now he is quite alone, single, without any member of the family. 'Dhungia' the strong smoke never act upon him. That strongness gives him the feeling of Mahuli gruel. He equated the crack of mango stone with the outbreak words of his emotion. Biswanath had let listened the howl in native language to the outsiders.

Hoo…t Nonsense.

The issue of Mango stone had been discussed like hot cake for the outsiders of Kasipur. We commemorate mango stone like so many things and so many festivals and fast. But there was shouting outside our village.

Desari does the work of astronomer by calculating planets to find out the auspicious and inauspicious things. He select about the marriage, Bahapuani. When there'll be tilling etc.? When there shall the field work be started? Desari decides and declare all about "Eating of new Mango products", we eat sweet tasty juiced full mango. Again Dissari calculate the auspicious date of celebration Rohinijoga. Then it brings the day of observation, "Stone festival", 'Taku Parva'. The canopy is hanged over to cover the place of celebration overhead. Eggs, flowers are placed on the canopy and the flours of mango stone is put under it, collected from each house of the village. Hand prepared wines were poured on the stone flour and Disari, the priest pour the blood of wrenched cocks head on that. The Dum dum sound of Drums and tree Drums multiply the moment of pleasure and merry making. Bejuni, the transgender dance along with music played by them. We end our celebration with this pump and luxury. We usually work hard for six months in field and the next six months doing nothing, sitting idle at home. The seasons of mango and jackfruit are completed in this way. The works of maze and mandia completed with this or that way. We didn't have grain for cooking rice, Mandu. That Mango stone flour save our lives at the time of scarcity, at the time of need. We keep our self busy in daily wages, kulikama and cultivation. Our maijes, wives, dokris, girls, they all together crack the stones for stone-celebration, Takuparva. They bring out soft portion out of that, dry them up, grind them flour to prepare them Jurum of gruel from that.

Searching was continued - who is Vijaya?

"I am Vijaya". Vijaya came and stood before them. Officers came from Bhubaneswar accompanied by the Collector of Raigarha, followed by the 'Hedu', head baboo of Laxmipur. Yes other five, but designations were not known. With wonder and gratefulness, Damba Barika, the talkative man of the tribal shouted, "Bada sahib has come, leave the works, come soon." Some of us went towards working place and others to attend the officers. But the officer came rushing to our people to talk to, by whisking his people. He consulted with the village chief, Maiji, women, Dokra Dokri, the girls to know about the reality. Then asked for our ration card. He recognised the residence of Dada sabat, the landlord of the village, when we denied for non-possession of ration card. Then inquired about his transactions and dealing with people. He was found most busy searching records, we had with us pitch of Salapa tree. He was in the state of drunk inebriate. He confessed all truth without break - "We don't have food to eat, it is only the gruel of mango stone and Katinga greens, we manage with that."

The officer nodded his head and had left the place assuring nothing. The Kuhalia, the talkative man of Kasipur had reached after four days. He was sizzled for drinking the black berry country wine from other village. He had carried his cycle on shoulder in rugged and uneven road but didn't take off that ever in plain road. Our Dhangdis, girls laughed, Kulukulu at him. He asked, "Where is Vijaya?" Vijaya came upon.

He accompanied some of our people and all had smoked 'Dhungia' and talked with them at the bank of Johola, a small stream, "That officer had already reported all about our matter to the government. The minister had confessed, some of them have been provided ration card but thjat cards were pledged with the village Mahajana, money lender, Dada Sabat. People did have rice to eat. Dada Sabat was supplied rice packet to give away to people but didn't do so. Here, the money lender, supplier and officers all have been unified to exploit you. "The work for food" has not begun yet in village. Let us see what happens next after this report."

Kasipuria went away. We were least concerned about the future consequence. But the crowd of outsiders were increasing in our village. They had kept us busy all times. Often, we spend our leisure times, just after drinking gruel and wine sitting on the Veramundi stone floor after coming back from cultivation. The floor of Veramani munda floor is the meeting place of our village, we seat and smoke Dhungia there. A lot of things are usually discussed there. Garudu Kandha speaks the history of old tradition, stories of hundred years back. He match and compare the past with present. There was no communication to our village, the alley of mountains. Danger, mountains stand everywhere. Sometimes Hedu, Garudu, RI visit our village to attack and size our cooked wine. Salti officer come to seize them. They are government, administrators. There was also premature death during those days. But no poison in air. Snats were there during those time. There was not many diseases by his stings.

When the road runs to our village, the outsiders such as Sundi, Telenga, Saukar, the money lender entered into our village. Sundi let our villagers drunkard by selling wines, and took all our properties. The leaders taking votes from us, they never come to village but make feast with country chicken and wine in the residence of Saukar. Saukar took their Bedha land. All our lands and crops were pledged with Telengana. The leaders give them contractor works, dealership and many profitable things. We are in the same Dark Age as before.

'Hai, Hai-yes… yes' we all support to Guruda. An old man of Laharikant had gone to Laxmipur with some works in blacksmith's manufactory and returned back with a message about the visit of MLAs to village. Political workers and officers from Kasipur and Raigada would come with the MLA's."

They all reached in a vehicle at our village Panasaguda. We saw the face of the MLAs after election. Mr. Krishna Mohapatra Sangram Dandasena and Jagdish Mohapatra of Kasipur all had come accompanied by MLAs. We stood before them with folding hands at the cost of our daily wages. MLAs hugged and had assured, "You'll have no problem further. I will arrange everything and take care of you."

Someone inquired, "Who is Viijaya?" Vijaya came rushing and stood in front. Krushna Mohapatra of Kasipur hid himself behind Bibhisana Majhi.

They went away. We went away for our daily work. Some Dhanda proceeded towards the bank of Jholakula. We cut our hairs of each other and we demonstrate the skill of hair cut with different styles. There was scissor's criss-cross sound. We love to live in tribe/ clan. We all know the skill of barber. We got a message on the way back to home after bathing in 'Jhola' that some people of Pitajholi village named Sindhe Majhi, Araju, Lekhana, Dalma Majhi all had turned up Duma, phantom one after another. Some of them were died of for want of food, some by eating poisonous food, some in disease and old age. There was mob and ferment of death by eating the flour of Mango stone, "Listen! How people were died of large degree, intimidate the death rate by numbers. Fifteen, twenty two - the news of death dance had made hue and cry outside Kasipur.

Perhaps, a wicked Duma was observing with wilfulness of our problems hidden on the top of any Danger. Somewhere the Evening star had peeped through our untimely sufferings. Who was that Duma brought as so many headache, we don't understand that.

Panel of doctors came to village and searched for the causes of deaths. They wanted to know the reasons of death due to different diseases. Who died of Maleria, purgation, dysentery or of any other reasons and gave away medicines to everybody. They scattered poisonous powder in Village Street and distributed glucose, neutral powder and Halogen tablets to purify the drinking water. The water pipe contractor had reached in village and repaired the non-functioning tubewells and repaired the rugged road with momrum hard soil. Some idle people were found to be excited to have heir exercise in our villages for our development.

The Dumbas declared in loud voice, "Head of the state will come to village. He will come to Therubali in Aeroplane. Then to Bilamala via Tikiriguda. The head comes accompanied by MLA, politicians, leaders, dealers and contractors, and officers. They had arrived and asked about Vijaya, "Where was he?"

He joggled the crowd to go front "I am Vijaya." But his voice was so low to be heard. The head was escorted by officers, heads and bodyguards to the vehicles.

Hills or Dungers were interlocked with each other around the village. The hills such as Kodingamali, Baflamali and Sasubahu are connected with each other with a little gap. Therubali, a small village is situated at the centre of these Dangers. All officers arrived in a aeroplane.

The phonograph of the flying insects and the sound of the aeroplane both are alike same, to us.

There was no sound in the night. The only sound that echoing the village was the cry of Biswanath Majhi's Maiji and his son at the death of his Dokri, the girl - "O Vijaya".

"Hai Kaka. Yes uncle", Vijaya responded. Vijaya didn't have sleep at all to his eyes. He had slept turning downward on the charpoy in prone in a lonely hut.

"Gyalpa, nonsense." Vijaya, you are the only matric plucked Dhangda of our village. Whosoever came, they all had asked about you. They made us silent and kept you witness. Will they ask you tomorrow? Will they come to your village again? Whatever thing they give away today, will they give them tomorrow? I am alone you too. If you are a worthy Dhanda, you come front or be at the corner of the room like Duma. Nonsense!

Vijaya was doodling and unsteady inside the lonely room and had exposed his body carelessly to the wild mosquito. The rats were running sacking Govt. Supplied rice packets.

There was an echo of coughing sound after smoking Dhungia. The whimping voice of his father and sobbing of his mother. Tini, Vijaya's sister's lament, as if all were adding to the thickness of dark night. He got up and dragged himself up towards the piles of mango stone where they, three Dumas : his father, mother and younger sister Tini were sitting together.

Their faces were very uncospicious in the smoke of Dhungia. The voice of his father was still very forceful and conservative as his son. Dhartini, the Earth has given birth a worthy daughter like Tini. The phantoms ran after them to beat both brother and sister. The God, Mahapru had covered the sun to darken the earth just to save the brother and sister. Both the children were floating on the boat made from silk cotton tree. The sun appeared on the sky after seven days. The earth became dried and the hills and mountains rose with their heads up. Forests were treading everywhere. They both became Dhanda and Dhandi. Then the God instructed Dhanda to carry on the family life. Get married to this Dhandi. Dhanda answered, "She is my sister." God had brought the disease small pox. The physical appearance of brother and sister were changed so they could not recognise each other. They began their family life becoming Docra and Dokri and had given birth seven sons. They were Miminika, Himerika, Hikoka, Praska, Muska, Zambka, Melaba. Each son formed a clan after his name. You are the up spring of that Miminika dynasty.

"Yes! This is Vijaya Miminika." Vijaya stretched hands towards them. That three Dumas were hidden in tenebros.

We usually forget the past. Someone, perhaps a Dhanda was playing a broken Gourd Guitar which was producing cracked tune Dung Dunga. There were many officers, photographers had been reaching at their village. A message had come how two Jhadiani of Jhadia villages breathed last. They were Suvarna Jhadiani and Ghas Jhadiani.

Some of them were striking their own chest - My

Duandi breathed last. The volunteers were reporting about the death rate with photo snaps. Perhaps they would extracted huge amount of money from any foreigner. During this crises, the opposite party leaders were giving away free kitchen facilities and shouted to give us food.

Last night, the Torch masal again lighted in the village again. Again we returned to village after bathing in Kajakada after cremation. We all villagers cried for his departure, as she had no one of her own to cry. That starved Duma made us moaning.

Some officers came in Kamani, and asked "Are all the Govt. Works done well? Where is Vijaya?" we took them to a hut. There was glow of sunshine overhead. The room was foggy like the smoke of Dhungia. The officer peeped into the dark foggy room.

As if Vijaya was sitting alive in the corner of the hut beside the pile of Mango stone. The rice packets cumulated upon one after other, tin of Kerosin, medicines all were upon each other, the free cooked rice and dal became stale and found mycelium growing on them.

MONKEY MEN

Rain cannot over take us. We are always in front line and rain just follows us behind.

We are advanced and expert. We can forecast the approaching rain. We move to construct a temporary camp. Rain follow us.

There is certain meaning and feelings of occasional raining in four months of rainy season. We stay temporary either in hut or in rivers belt or on any unfertile land. Rain comes dancing forcefully, no fear of breaking of huts. Rain may paly and chintz to make us wet but we will not get wet completely. If we stay in the place where there is any possibility of heavy down pour but we don't stay there; we could never mistaken reading the intention of rain. If there is down pour for two days or three days and there to storm and that keep us quite disturbed, old people instruct to shift the village. Then we all the clans load all our daily useful things from small to big and carry them to another place. Rain abated completely but cannot reach us.

Our forefathers have cursed the rain and they have done the same in return. Don't possess a home or village. Migrate from place to place homeless and without village.

We move very comfortable continuously without exhaustion. There was dense forest. There was lot of honey.

Now there is no tree. There must be mining or industrial areas. We observe how the tribal people work in the mines and become babu like urban people.

We have no change, we can't engage ourselves in daily wages but the only work, weaving of mats drinking of Tadi, the home prepared wine, taddy and eating of monkey's flesh and so on. These are our pleasure.

We cannot accommodate ourselves with the tribal people living beside the National Highway or the native Odia people live in our surrounding. But we are with our 'Emphi' all times to come and will support all times. Without any hesitation.

We are neither Odia nor tribal Adivasi. People say, the entire world is crying and express her sorry as we the sub-tribal community are about to extinct. Foreign funds are funded regularly to us. That Empi is taking care of that funding we are discussed, debated in Delhi only for Mphi.

We are least concerned what to us, if people discuss us. We have already told to Emphi O respected sir. You please take care you give us cloth, Nuga; you may give us food if you like to help us sometimes. You must take care of us whenever you find leisure time. ask about our problems. You must be searching for us in mines area, villages. Wherever we wander or go no matter, we will come to caste our votes at the times of election. But one of our requests not to build any pucca house for us, if you do, ghosts will live there not your men. As you know we don't stay in a particular place or a particular area for long time. We love to live in hut. We love to live with our clan, to live with our own people is greater than living else where. We have promised for our Emphi (MP). Our word is our action. Our thoughts and actions are both same. We never understand either Congress or BJP or Communist parties; we are with our Emphi. We follow him.

Emphi told that his son would contest this year in the place of his father. He will do new works for you. We told, Sir! We don't know your son. If he won't give any new garment. We are least concerned. He may not give us feast sometimes. But he must care for us. He will come to us. He will take care of us after coming from Delhi. Works-jobs are not problem for us. We are gifted two hands for wearing mat. If we have nets for monkeys that is enough for us.

Emphi knows about us very well. We know one man, we are obstinate. Emphi told to caste vote to his son. He will take care of you as I'm to you.

Thus, our vote will go to him. We declared that forceful response. The MP has dined feast with us. Drank Toodi upto brim. He danced nude in intoxication in full moon night with us. He falsely attracted to us. Used slang, quarrelled with us. Then laughed and made us laughed then went back home in midnight.

The same thing is repeated next day. The pleasure of the previous night never continue till next day. Some of us cut date leaves climbing the date palm tree. Dry them up and weave mat particularly old people are engaged with that. Girls colour them and dry up when the sun shines heat the morning shine. Young boys becomes stone. The throats of the young males are dried up. When we sit under the shed of the trees of unfertile land, we use to talk about monkeys. We feel ourselves mad if we talk about money. The scene f monkey becomes invisible to us. We don't value the worth of the village without monkeys. We hate that village. We motivate the olds to leave the place for other village. Where the availability of water facility is there. There must be date palm trees and small bazar nearby. So, there will be good transaction of salpa mats.

The old people could understand the young's gesture. They're acting like us in their youth. They were migrating from one place to another place becoming mad after monkeys.

Thus there is not any permanent inhabitation of our. It is always changed. We all move together in group. We make temporary inhabitation in open and unfertile field. And there must be a bazar, water facility, agriculture field a bit away from our living places. Sometimes the monkeys come one after another in noon. We admit that village where all facilities are available. After arrival from Delhi the Emphi, he comes to us where ever we stay. His son, after became Emphi in place of his father never behaves us equally like his father. Now-a-days our net never catches any monkey. Moneys like our new Emphi, never comes to us perhaps at the smell of our body.

An Emphi was defeated contesting with our Emphi. Later he came on a bike and reminded that see! Father MP had a regular touch with you, but the son Emphi was exploiting the Govt. fund and funds of foreign country. He consumed everything. His son became Emphi but he does not have any contact with us. If you want to cast your vote, you please give to me. I will take care of you.

We answered, "We are one, our father is one, our opinion is one. We can't bend down our heads if the son changes his direction. We won't change our opinion."

Then he went away. Yes! He has come to motivate us to become Emphi, nonsense.

Once, our anger had reached on the climax. A labour-leader came to collect subscription; as we had made our temporary residence in mine's area. The real problem was the rain and the tempest followed us, we ran and shifted our village ot the safest area of mines. That labour-leader taught us many things. He came and drank toodi with our youths. He made friendship with us and gave us advice through scolding. Hey nonsense. People of foolish community. People carry politics with your community. You are the vote bank. They became Emphi for your favour. They become rich for you. You remain as the same laterite stone forever. You stupid, arise, awake, so that the exploitation could be removed. You all try to become the members of our Trade union. This union will run after you.

The intoxication of Toodi rose to our head. We told if you all maintain yourselves taking money from workers then what's wrong if the Emphi become rich with our money. What right you have to say against our leader. We don't understand anything about union and funion; our Emphi is our union and our institution.

He got annoyed in our statements - you stupid, monkeys you try to become educated and wise. You nonsense, gaja-elephant try to understand. Dynamite will be dropped on you. Dynamite - waiting for you. Wait.

He left grumbled, our laughter followed him. We feel pleasure laughing at the attitude of the politicians. We feel one thing, our leader, the Emphi sir was good to us. It is a special kind of pleasure to mock the leaders in their absence. We know one thing. We became harass when his son became Emphi. He is good. All other leaders are thieves. The toxication of toodi creates drowsiness. The sister-in-law in relation jokes with us on the way back home, carrying their water pots on heads. Dear brother-in-law! have you all become date palm trees? The sister-in-law mock. Our drowsiness and intoxication of toodi wine broke down and dissapeared. What nonsense, the women the Tirlas joked with us. Wake up. Let us prove if we are date palm trees or vigorous males. Some of skewed and obstinate youngs of us go rushing into the slum and carry their dry wood fuel billet. A song of hunting tune raised with high sound in our groups. We the youngsters of four group move to four direction. The middle group is termed as Daka-Dal or loudspeaker group. They call shouting. The game of lurking Chhaka Chhaki - watching to each other-climb up trees and coming down - criss cross running undoubtedly we come upon a prey in the meantime with engagement of these activities. We reach with a big bowel full mutton to the in law who played joke with us. Red colour soap and meaty flavour we the group of young in laws take revenge of our anger and tell, "We the date-palm trees have come with meat curry. O listen! And take this curry from us."

We all the sister in laws and brother in laws usually involve in fondness with each other. And there is conflicts and quarrel takes place in between young and old men commonly. The young grand daughters convince the old men and old women to youngsters to settle down the problems. This is usual habits in between the young and old people. We may live without food for two days but pleasure and joke in leisure is common to our tribe. We value the worth of living in this way.

The old Emphi was regularly visiting us. But his son is not coming regularly. This attitude hurt us and make us sad. In spite of that, we don't have any repentance for this indifference. We have profound faith upon us. Rain cannot overtake us. Can't go ahead of us. Neither the Odia nor the Adivasi tribal are well to condition better than one thing. If we change the place that should be within the area of Emphi. If any problem arises, our Emphi will take care of that. But our youngsters want to go to new places - hunt new preys -

come upon new people and new business will be done. But old people, they are very thoughtful and caring about this. Once, one of the young man brought black goggles, black suit and printed shirt and put on that, the old people opposed that and warned "Why are you wearing the dress of Odia?" Nonsense. You try to becoming humorous.

On the other day one of our young's make friendship with Adivasi and danced in their Makara festival and rolled on the road after drinking Toodi. All the old persons were got angry - Nonsense becoming Adivasi. Drinking Handia wine. Then, he will keep concubine-Reja after this. He will ruin our community at last.

All our modernity has been arrested within the conservative visions of our youths. The skills of hunting, net-catching and wearing of mats are all the technique of our hands.

Famine fell upon us that year. Costs of the commodities had increased in leaps and bound. There was not good business of mat. Starvation and sufferings became the matter. We chocked out this plan and programme with drinking state of Toodi - someone asked to know about Emphi. Why this problem of us are not published in newspaper. Is he not reading the newspaper about us in Delhi? His father reached before us all times at the time of need but where has he gone? We seek his presence at the time of starvation. We become distress.

Sometimes we utter him salle at the time of famish. We just can't escape after scolding him. Our olds may lying in death bed but they can't tolerate the scolding to Emphi. The old men grumble on us why you rebuke to Emphi? The giver of our food. We were eating salt from his father. You just endure this thing. The Emphi is young. He has been to Delhi fresh. He will certainly come at the time of vote. The olds express their anger like old monkeys sometimes their predictions appears to be true. Emphi usually come to us after long days. He didn't have idea about our starvation and famine. He pays attention on our approach of requests and express his deep regrets for our sufferings and keep two bundles of notes. Our anger and sulk disappeared immediately. The thoughts of dancing vibrate us within. We urge to fell on his feet and beg pardon, "Pardon sir. We have scolded you. Grumbled upon you."

Emphi laughs... "OK... OK, You are all my men. Aren't?"

This new Emphi is very open minded. Thus, not complicated and reserved like his father. We express all our thoughts before him - vomit everything but we remain silence in toxication of toodi. If our talking will be derailed. The old men comments. Look now observe what types of good man is he. He gave us a lot at once but his father was giving this amount in four to five instalments. Compare the father with his son.

Emphi was trying to tell, "I have come to you for a special work. His followers were standing close to him. They hinted the Emphi to expose that later. Sir, they must be waiting for us in the meeting. Urgent. Emphi became hurried. Don't be sad. I will come to you again. You have to do a work. You will be popular and famed for that.

We paid our regards expressing sir and sir Emphi left for urgent meeting. We forgot everything. We assumed that Emphi is with us in every problem. He will certainly come to us.

Whenever any occasion comes - Thakurani Parava or any day of observance. We distributed that money as per head. Then we drink Toodi upto brim - go for hunting and merry make with pleasure.

Days are passed like anything for these small affairs. We forget our sorrows. Yes everything is ok. But we are very aggressive by nature. If any one get us angry, we go to any extend. We became obstinate. Once, one of us motivated a girl and said, you have preserved everything. Why don't you like to offer it?

Ay! Are you asking like Odia young man about love? Or, you live like Adivasi young man? You have no stamina the net nor strength Hmm... demonstrating strength! becoming wile.

That girl was very clever - she responded on pace. He was afraid of hearing the respond of the girl and bathed in sweating. That boy has come rushing to our group and pretended. We encouraged him. You join in our group first and cooperate us in netting. Watch the net. Learn how to hunt, drink toodi, Hurt prey. Do hard work. Then she will cooperate you.

This is the technique to increase the number of the group. We may have fraction in group but we unite ourselves at the time of daily wages and hunting. Our old man they have been living in group traditionally. Let the olds not to criticise us. Group grow like tree because we never break the group.

Rain always follows us. In the mean time we have changed our place and migrated to another place. After long search Emphi has reached at our place. No follower was with him except the driver.

When Emphi got down from the vehicle we all gathers around him. He told, he could not stay with us for long time. You must have learned a dance. Let us have it. We all will drink and dance together. Let me come tomorrow. Yes tomorrow better than today.

Tomorrow Emphi comes. He will dance with us like

his father, He will be friendly with us. There will be celebration of Toodi. There will be hunting. We the youngsters became very much emotional. The olds reminded us about Emphi's arrival and the news removed all our enjoyment. Have all your experienced dance. Emphi will see your dance tomorrow.

Some of us danced film dance like drunkard. The olds gave remark that these stupids are dancing like Odia. Then some of us danced holding each other by waists.

Again, the olds commented us that these nonsense are dancing like wild Adivasi. Listen! Our dance is not at all like their dances; we have our special dances. Emphi will see this and give us prize.

Have you taught us our dance? None of our fathers or forefathers have taught us this dance. First let us have a demonstration by you?

This comment irritated and nudged the olds of our community, perhaps; it striked to their sentiments. Having heard this an effeminate of his fifties who was sitting on the log, had jumped to mid of us. He chatter and laid on the floor and danced like four footed monkeys. He turned up to back and made a face showing his broken teeth. Then scratched his body like monkeys. He searched louse, climbed tree then jumped from branch to branch. Warmed up exercises and showed different actions of monkey.

Some of us shouted. Hey! this must be monkey dance. Yes! Monkey dance. We the youngsters joined our hands with that effeminate man, jumped like monkey. Some of us danced in half drunk of fully drunk state. We all became happy that we have learned the dance of our own culture and performed that we continued our dance and we became conscious of our customs. We felt very tired. Emphi comes tomorrow. He will dance, drink. We will hunt. All were decided, tomorrow.

We have no idea of complacency. We have this much knowledge of weaving net to open and how to spread the net to trap the monkeys and leaders.

We are condemned for hunting. Let us know whether the Adivasis are eating goat, cows, pigs, sheep etc. or not? Are the Muslims not eating cows or not? We hunt an animal to eat. Aren't Odias eating goat or hens? People should not comment on foods of others. We have been acquainted with a particular type of food. That is our favourite food. We do hard labour for that. We hunt the prey and eat and hiccup after eating. All that ceremonies of marriage, celebrations of festival and fast become disinterested if there is not prey. Yes! The prey is found in villages or we run to all distance directions to find them. It needs a company, togetherness for a prey. Interest and willingness mind set is required for preying. When we gather our equipments such as nets, harpoon, carrier stick, we forget everything. No human being is visible but the monkeys at the time of hunting. It needs to dissuade the male monkey from the group. Otherwise it would fight with us not let a single female monkey Mahuvi monkey to be trapped, sometime Ape must be hanging below the belley of the female Mahuli. We have to dissuade them from all directions for smooth preying. We only choose, fatten female Mahuli for our prey. Circle or gherat is made with net, we carry the prey by carrying stick, Bahungi, leeing the Odia people's sight. Then the neck of the preys are cut and flay. Our people shovel to take the thighs, some of us demand for liver and heart but the grand share is kept for the young hunter those who have returned from hunting. This way or that, the share of meat or saguati is made by us. The portion of share go to others. That lays the young people. All the young people will dance drinking Toodi up to brim, intoxicated.

The old people remain mum. They know that the lion portion of the meat will go to young. They were acquainted with this habit since their childhood. They recollect their past days, about their boyhood desperado. All that magic words are printed in our blood.

Our feast is organised with great pleasure. Just as our happiness for hunting. We try for the feast with the Emphy sir with merry making grand success. All the youths, olds, effeminates will dance monkey dance with Emphi sir. Some of us we will be divided for cooking hunting. We made a group for different works.

The olds started leading the activities. They warned, "Don't drink too much that day, there may be imbalance in between words and actions." The young educated Emphi is not uneducated like his father ex-Emphi. Listen! All the girls, women of the village will be addressed by the leaders. Get cleaned the houses. Emphi may stay with us tomorrow.

We forget everything, sleep disappear from eyes. If there is any responsibility fixed upon us. The plans of prey of next days dance in our eyes, feast of the jag is done. Emphy is not certainly with this dream. That is our pleasure, our plans and programmes. Sometimes this thing keep us busy and sleepless in night. The oldman act mystify before the old woman, this act made us more romantic and more colourful. Ladies decorate braid and lace. Deploy the grand daughter in work. Let the Emphy sit on our Mat, get the weave of that standard.

Two passed, Grand daughters were busy in conversations. This Emphy is young his father was old haggards. Black like pig. This young one is of white complexion. Straight like banana plant.

The younger sister makes jokes and wants to know, could my brother-in-law become banana plant. But my brother-in-law is very cunning like all our youngs. Babana ghost, stupid, all laugh. Night passed intoxication.

Again, there runs the show of training of monkey dance in morning. The Effiminate, shows her dance like a skillful trainer. He recollects his childhood affairs, the way he had learned the dance and training, he acted in that way. And he let the youngs dance with him. Sometimes youngs let the effeminate learn education from them. If anyone learned the dance of new technology, he teaches others this dance. This is the dance. Some of us caricatured the actions of the monkeys. The new variety of dances are also added to the old dance. Above all there was an art of monkey dance in our blood.

Mid-day is suitable for hunting. But that day all our young men prepared for hunting with net early in the morning.

All women were waiting for the vehicles' sound and for the arrival of the Emphi sir. If there is any sound, that must be Emphi's vehicle. We had forgotten all our sufferings of monkey hunting of the whole day and that was disappeared when Emphi sir arrived and sat down on the floor in date-mat.

Emphi asked, have you got prepared yours monkey dance well?

We said, Yes! Sir.

Have you done your prey today or not? Emphi asked. The young one who had preyed monkey answered enthusiastically and overwhelmingly, yes! Sir.

Then we will have feast and get together today.

We danced within at this statement of the Emphi. Yes! Sir.

Emphi sir called someone close to him and stretched a hundred rupees note and hold, you get arranged country chicken for me. I have brought foreign liquor for you all. Today you may stop drinking Toodi for today. You take each a cigarette. All snatched away cigarette each. A young man journeyed in search of country chicken with that hundred rupees. I have come to befriend with you, after a sip of wine, to dine with you, to drink with you like my father did have with you.

All toon sips drought of foreign liquor. The toodi drinking lips of our sensitised with the sipping of foreign liquor. We gazed at Emphi. All drums and music equipment would be provided to you for your musical group, dresses too. All the expenditures of communication, fooding and lodging will be borne by the government. We will take you to Delhi.

If we dance that monkey dance, its for you, but not for Delhians, one of the obstinate youngs had argued with Emphi. The old avoided and warned not to argue with Emphi sir. What do you think of our Emphi sir? You feel it heaven.

Emphi hugged the drunkard young man and convinced him. See! There is a lot of Emphies in Odisha. They take dance party from Bhubaneswar and demonstrate that performances by naming them Dance of Kalahandi, Sambalpuri and Kataki etc. I thought myself backward in this race. You are my people, why should not I take benefits. The rural dancers visiting to foreign. Are you afraid of Delhi? Let us go to Delhi.

The Effeminate and his young actors gave their consent to go to Delhi. Again dance started for this work. All drank wine. Emphi asked, "Let me see your dance. Effeminate shouted, "Come up."

Wonderful! They started the violent dance. Emphi was overdrank and became overwhelmed and he danced like monkey too.

Some were engaged in cooking, some in listening and others in drinking - all were whimsy and unconscious.

There was old man. Worn out in old age. Sitting in dark corner isolately, alienating himself from such pleasant moments waiting for hunting meat. One young man looked and went rushing towards that direction. O Mahapru old man, "Why are you sitting in swelling face. Are you not happy with our happiness? Are they not suit you?"

No that is not. I was lost in deep thought. There will be rain within two days. May be calamities. I smell that. Have you seen loo wind in midday, as if my nose chocked in rain wind. Rain is running after us. Shift the tent tonight. Leave this place.

This whispering spread from ear to ear. Rain is coming soon. Storm is approaching. The great disaster is approaching. A havoc spread and all became hurried to shift the village. The intoxication cracked like anything. Monkey dance faded like autumn leaves.

Whatever it may be, the rain can't overtake us. We are always ahead of rain. Rain just follow us.

We know this memorable night with the Emphi may not repeat tomorrow. We are like this happiness climb to the climax and the same may disappear immediately. We know afraid of anyone.

The only afraidness i.e. rain. Some of us will go to Delhi for dance. Emphi may come for other works. The effeminate old man and his dancers will exploit us by the name of Emphi. This community, this unity will be fractioned.

The cook declared the completion of cooking. Two young went rushing to the kitchen place.

We know about rain. Emphi will be see off after the feast. We will shift ourselves to new place with our bag and bagges. But Emphi was sitting with empty plate. He was talking out of intoxication. Understand. I will take this party to Delhi. Then I will make a lobby to send them abroad. You will board the aeroplane for foreign. You will see the entire world.

Cooked meats were piled in two places of kitchen. There was Monkey's meat for us in big place. The small pile was for Emphi with country chicken.

Two young men went for fetching the food which was delaying unnecessarily. Rice was already served. All were waiting for meat in up head. The olds could predict the matter inside though they were in dinning place.

An old man shouted. O' two nonsense Abaincha. Are you tasting meat inside? Bring quickly. It becomes late for our sir. Rain is following us.

Some of us were whispering well! Is the young Emphi like his father? Okay. His father drink toodi with us. If he drank foreign liquor with us. Does not matter. He fed us foreign liquor. Its good. Still, he made friendship with us. Gave us heart. Gave us company. No matter if he hated our Toodi. We hunted with a lot of pain. His father was eating dinning with us without any hesitation. But he made special arrangement with country chicken with us.

Rain is thundering. People are shouting for meat. Our young servers exchanged the meat bowel in kitchen.

PARTY'S PARTY

I, not with others help but with my own effort, have already located the place where Dasuram of Gurudipanka lives. Dasu appears very thin simple and fool but very clever singer. Dasuram, the poet.

Actually, I was running with bad times, body blow. There was a serious meeting at Mandimera forest had already been arranged for a hot discussion about my affairs of love with a girl of party's scard. They had decided that we should wait for at least one year, if we really had any intention of marriage. I thought it was better to be constrained.

Working in a party implies to love, no alternative to lead a life or die in lamentation. There is certain principle of the party organisation. No problem, if you want to carry the family life, but issues undoubtedly a big problem. Say no to children.

If there will be complicacy in party's development, in anticipation that after waiting for a year, she was sent to the border of Andhra Pradesh. I was stepped down from the troop of Gurritha and removed gun from my shoulder. I was ordered to take care of mass-contact cultural programme of the district of Gajapati and Raigada.

Actually, being a philosopher, the philosophy of

others become ineffective on me, just as Mao Tse Tung. I have already, got by heart his philosophy being one of the party's members. Indeed, to defeat the enemies, we have to depend upon the people having their guns of their own, not to be dependant absolutely. We need a cultural party along with this thought - which will help us to unite all together. In quest, I came upon a party at Gurudipanka village - the party of Dasuram.

I, in Adaba forest was sitting for five to six days lonely at the hut of Soura-tribal man. Thoughtful state kept me confused how and with whom should I start my project. Junus, the informer of the party arrived, he had a small dream to act in the party with a rifle and in dress. He works mindfully to fulfil his desire.

He, that Junus, for the first time gave news about Dasuram Maleka. "What is he doing now?", I asked him. He is doing his regular work; very poor boy with standard seven education. Composing songs, and has formed a music party, attend every programme in village and nearby villages, be it marriage, parting of bride, Dasuram reaches there. His father is bedridden. His mother, wife, the only members of his family.

My inquisitiveness to know about Dasuram made me enthusiastic. I, from Junus, the informer wanted to collect all datas about Dasuram.

There, the village watchman is treated as government. His opinion is considered as order of the government. If the village street becomes muddy, he imposes fine on people whatever amount he utter, people will have to pay him. Why you two brothers quarrel with each other drinking pay twenty-five rupees. Forest guard comes and collect one rupee for each cow and ox and fifty rupees for goat. If fails, arrest is a most. Ward member takes money for old age pension, money will have to pay for BPL ration card for the expenses of paper work and processing fees. Kumutis, money lenders are Govts. for them.

I, nictitate everything from Junus all about Dasu. He had not taken the charge of unification of rebellions of entire villagers. Some supporters were needed for the prosperity of that party. There was not any instruction from party to reach at village. He couldn't decide whether he should meet Dasuram or not. I, prepared a letter for my commander. I, told Junus to communicate him immediately, if the party of Dasuram comes for any programme to any village. I urge to come upon that Kuwi poet. I need to know him. If he is in place of dispute no matter, then I will meet him, otherwise escape.

I longed for Dasuram to call on him. Quite personal matter that has to deal with was making me unsteady. When the entire village went for sleeping, I trod on dried sal leaves in catwalk, remember my love, mine waiting for a year, I shallow the pain of castration.

In one early morning, Junus came with a news - there was a programme to be held at Adaba jangar Kuwi village. Dasu attends that song and dance programme on Friday night.

It may be 8 or 9 O' clock in night time, with the tune of cricket and insects, I entered into the forest to reach at that village. The melody of the distance Kuwi's song and dance was wafting in air, they were the mixed thrilling voice of tambour and ghungur riwaz and chorous. I could recognise him in the crowd of the party. The man, who was leading the song and in appearance was short, frail, black colour, playing changu, the tambour. He must certainly be Dasuram.

The youngs dhangda and dhangdi start singing and

dancing by holding the waist of each other, if Dasu's voice becomes tire. He was sitting in semi darkness and observing the dance and song - Junus came and whispered that people of the party have come, they wanted to talk to you.

I was sitting on the yard of Digambar Das came and paid regards bending his head. 'Babu Juhar.'

Be seated Dasu. I let him sit beside me by holding his hand. Are you writing poems of marriage, parting of the bride and festivals. Don't you write any new songs? Your Kuwi people will be courageous, they will be changed. Why don't you do that?

Dasu grasped my intention, the gravity of my suggestion. "Do you mean revolutionary song?" I have composed songs of that theme. But I have not sung anywhere. I have got a book of Klemanta Nayak, the man of Phulbani district "Kuwidin Punga", my songs are of that type. I, being inspired by his writing, have composed songs like that "Gajapati Jila tade suna / Gajapati dina Tade muan / Mandarwaku nanche suna/ Raba nanju ine nade munan."

Sir, I know, Hindi, English, Odia, Telegu language. I have also acquired certain knowledge on tribal Kuwi, Soura language. There was satire on the establishment of Dasu appealed me, I hugged him.

Dasu, for his creation of Kuwi language and for emotional songs of encouragement and he accused that - the first enemy of our Kuwi language are our own people. The low caste, Damb and schedule caste people of our community who have been baptised to become Christians, they are told by fathers and sisters of the church not to do, dance, song sacrifice of cock as that activities are not permissible in our community. Our Jesus will get angry, if do your cultural activities in our religion. You surrender yourself to Jesus not to anyone. Pray him in morning and evening. Some of us like Hindu wear sacred thread and playing their bhajan and prayer. They perform Hindu festivals and fasts, drink mahuli and dance pacing with the tune of the song. Let me know, will there be any existence of our culture and tradition?

I watch Dasu's conversation. I could observe, this Kuwi man who has lost himself in the song, dance, language, fast and festivals of Kuwi community. I could distinguish his dream and visions for future, for the prosperity of Kuwi communities and pulsating of hot blood.

We convince them, you may convert yourself to any religion, we have no objection but don't give up your own culture, song, dance, rejoicing etc. if you don't, it will disappear. We are Adivasi, tribals. We have our own religion. It is only money lenders and government are dividing us into parts of Hindu and Christian.

That black, thin, short Kuwi man's talks was very energetic, forceful and fighting spirit. I wanted to know from him, what other works he did, when there was no programme of song and dance.

How could I say, sir the work I do is certainly for the benefit of my villagers a kind of service, sir. I want to change their attitudes, their mind sets, their ignorance. I want them to be clever and educated. We take care of their development.

What do you say to them?

We educate then not to depend upon nicromancy, why tiger will eat us? Why there is no necromancer in landlords house. If any witch-doctor comes to our village, we dissuade him. We convince them, if anyone suffer from fever take quinine. Don't sacrifice cock or invite with-doctor. I have composed songs on this matter too.

I showed my interest to know much. In our custom, there is a system of 'Kenda' or dowry what the groom has to pay to the bride. In dowry, we give, cattle, oxen, cows, brass utensils to the groom, which becomes more difficult on the part of groom. In past, if any dhanda is not paid 'Kenda', he has to pledge and surety himself as bonded labour in the father in law's house or in bride's house. Sometimes, the groom go outside as bonded labour to pay bride price. To eradicate this superstitious beliefs from society, we convinced them to accept the system of love marriage. Let the groom give some lumsum amount to groom. That system is also a problem. At length, we have abolished that thing completely and adopted love marriage. No one pays nothing to no one. Slowly it has been occupied to our system.

Dasu's intelligence became effective to bring back people from superstitious thoughts. The jaw of his face was exposed that made his face loony beside the sunken check and flashing eyes. I, just stimulated him, "The village watchman is your government?" first, you stop people going to police staton for complaint. Settle all disputes here, so that the exploitation of police and watchman's will be stopped. No threatening, no income.

Yes! You are absolutely right sir.

I have heard, the Kumuti, money lender, wine shop all are powerful here. You convince people, if you want to drink, get prepared it and drink. Don't drink by surety your land and utensils to the wine shop owner. You plant bark tree and collect bark wine in it. Give away to others. Don't drink buying it, you break the energy and diplomatic attitude of Kumuti and Sandi, the money lender and wine shop owner.

I was over loading these burdens on the head of Dasu like a true comedian of the party. I, just tried to replenish some courage of determination for doing something. Dasu, for the downfall of his forefathers for drinking wine, suffer with a lot of pain. Sir, I compose songs to aware of our people against wine. On the spot, Dasu began to sing the lines :

You went to burial ground
Sold all your possessions and father
Patches of land of fore fathers
And the valuable properties
Gold silver, what not, did for wine
Showing your aristocracy
Rising up your moustache
Declaring yourself rich
But wear torn clothes
Wander like a dirty man
Not repairing thatched
Prefer staying at home
Both the sun and the moon
Enter freely into room
Who drank wine - His wife went for bonded labour
Who drank wine - He grab money from his spouse
Became inebriated, who drank
Took live of his wife,
Surety in landlords house
Pledged himself in money lender's house.

The voice of Dasu was filled with a traditional conservation and wild thought of retaliation of the past. Boys of the party, dozing now and then, came together after broke up their sleep. They started riaz, matching their voices with the voice of Dasu. That continued till morning. "Bhorku Kale matbar."

When the programme is over, they will go back to Gurudipanka. I selected Dasu, among them all. You write poem for your people - you fight for them too. The association of farmers and daily wagers are doing all works for them in the district of Raigada and Gajapati. Be a member of that association. They can cooperate you how to organise a union and what type of songs would you write? Then you will become a fighter.

Okay sir, I will be a member.

Dasu was the only M.E. standard man of Gurudipanka. He could sense the gravity of becoming member. He promised to be penniless and poor for the development of Kuwi people. He too made up his mind to jump into fire for Kui people. He made himself busy to leave Adaba village to catch the footway with his music party to reach at Gurudipanka.

A big body - blow may come in the life of the Kuwi poet after this. I predicted, there will be certainly danger and problems arise in the life. He will be rectified for betterment. He will be more stronger and stronger.

News conveyed to me, I have to leave for Raigada from Gajapati.

The commander, I felt, perhaps must be transferring me from one place to other place, in view of not to let me marry, as I was awaiting for that since long. In Andra Odisha border, my love, who is fighting in Gurella across the Andra.

I lament for my love in such a time that, I have to suffer like anything in her absence.

I brought out a four-folded love letter from my pocket, what I had written three to four months ago, but not found any messenger to send it her. I still search for that messenger for delivery of that letter, but found not such reliable man. Once, Birpa, the informer gave me a message that a messenger has come to Merimenda named Suvarao. I left everything back and ran rushing to Meramendi. I do admit, we the lovers consume some times for writing letters for our beloved, think a while, this is against the party's principle, still we consume times for our dear one.

I, reread that old letter again before, it slipped out from my hand. I found that useless when I swept my eyes over that writings. I couldn't predict, which day, it will touch the fingers of my love, it may take months together or no certainity of receiving this. But from the time, I delivered the letter, I became emotional and enthusiastic to find the answer of my letter. It becomes intolerable to wait for her. It is better to surge the interest. The fear of cubuctomy, pinching my heart since long days. In moon lite night, at the time of wandering in forest, if a dry leaf dropped down, I feel falling of my penis. Sweat flow like water. Such thought perspire me.

One lesson, we all have learned, to work hard, to walk on hard path, try to kill your enemy, if fail kick to his belly, you get yourself prepared mentally and physically to confront any harass situations.

Yes! I am ready.

The letter that has put my mind in tension, let me finish that first. I torn that old letter before Savarao and wrote a new letter. I have made up my mind to complete the operation work within two months right now. I think to give full stop to that incomplete work after your arrival, I will apply for leave from party. "Lal Salam", Red regards.

He handed over letter to Suvarao, some extend that act reduced the tension from my mind and half of the fear for vesctomy disappeared instantly. I bound the bag and baggages, my camp from Gajapati to Raigada.

The work about the mass-contact programme that allotted to me, moving from confined to forest on foot, makes me bore and disinterest, solitary confinement. When I decide to stay one night with any Adivasi-tribal family, the short hult with the members usually gives me a feelings of staying like with my own family. I'm doing work for my own family, a kind of attachment and feelings of responsibility hunts my mind.

During a stay for long time at the residence of Srinu, in the village Pandratala, a message I got that there committee of farmers was going to be formed and daily wagers to which Dasuram was invited.

Why should I sit here silently? Let me know, how much Dasuram, the Kuwi poet has progressed in composing stimulative songs? How much he has burnt to himself? How much he has let others burn? I should go to that place, where Dasu comes to make his programme. Let me examine and enjoy the song of Dasuram.

It became night at Kolnara, after walking twelve kms distance in the forest with Srinu. There was a meeting of farmers and daily wagers committee, going on in the jack tree orchad. The party commander of Raigada zone and members of the neighbouring village had come to attend the meeting. There should not be leakage of any secrecy of the party, the distribution of responsibility and about the future plan and programme, discussion were on serious mood. The hot discuss on political situations of Gunupur and the agitation of lands to Gudari was going on. The turn of Dasu came. He was called upon.

Dasu inned banian in green colour folded loongi and red turban on head responded the call by standing up with folding hand. That frail and thin black colour youngman picked up his tambour on to chest. He broke the silence of Kolnara forest by his stimulative enchanted Kuwi song and music

> "This region and this Kuwi language
> Come, make a chain, be unite for this
> Come, all the community of Raigada
> Gajapati and Phulbani come, O' come

> Let us unite ourselves, make tie
> Form an association.
> Come O' come all Kui people
> To fulfil out aim success
> Be unite all deprives
> Demand our claim on our forest
> Our birth right, forefathers property
> Let us rise up hands
> Won't let others kick
> On our belly on our foods.

The hot song of Dasu attracted a demand for another song next the present one. Dasu sharpened and cleared his voice. He mixed his hot breathing with the web of the song. The frail young Dasu waved his old song "Bedanda Govt." nonsense government

> O' betrayal government,
> O' Police thieves, docait
> All're touts, all're
> Ministers, king, councillors
> Not a single man gentle here
> Take all our pet cocks
> Nothing requests are heard
> No attention to sad
> Dogs're the police guards
> Be unite, all the deprives
> Be one all the sufferers
> Let us fight against them
> Till our goals are reached
> Pay regards to all you needs.

In the song, the feelings of hatredness and disregards filled against the standing government. The gathered, Kuwi, souras were dancing at the tune of music and song of

Dasuram. In support and response to the song, the enraged audience rose their arrows and bows, axes, hatchets up. The fighting fiery song, amidst it, Dasu was standing on burning fire. During the time of coming back to Gajapti, I came upon Dasu and enquired, "If all things are doing well in that area or not?"

"I should not tell, all the goings are well", I'm in the eye of Meramundi police station, as I am writing songs for farmers, singing them in different programmes," said Dasu. They compel Dasu to stop writing songs they threaten, they instructed to stop everything. Why should I stop writing and singing of songs? They may say. I don't pay any attention. They may say but I will do my work at whatever cost. If they say me to leave village. Shall I do that. I can't do what they say.

Dasu's temperament appealed me a lot. I realised that his preliminary education of the party has already been started. He has made strong his party. In the meantime Dasuram has become the convenor of the Raigada's farmers association.

About Dasuram one of the situation of the boy hood I recollected. Once, Dasu came upon an animal shallowed a man half on the feet of the mountain, Danger while he himself was walking on the hill. He had never come upon such type of creature before. Villagers couldn't believe Dasu's description of peculiar type of creature. Other day, both Suvash and Dasu were wandering in forest, all on sudden, Dasu found the same creature and climbed up tree out of fear. Suvash criticised him, fool, "That is not a motor jeep, the man inside the jeep is the driver, look half outside."

One day, the man who had a fear for jeep, now the same man become the convenor of the farmer association. Here, a word of voltire strided to my mind, "Revolution is an egg." I went one step advance and thought, that egg has been hatched a chicken which has seen the sun's light - He is Dasuram.

Moreover, the party recruits some talents among the Kuwi, Soura, Kandha, Santhal children and to train them up to become comred of the party. I remember the first day of training in the party how to fire the rifle? How to deliver motivated fiery speech? How to learn the language of Adivasi? How to do hard labour to stand us by yourself? All the warnings, all the information and skills and techniques for the party. You incessantly supposed to carry the gun on your shoulder, whether you are defecating or eating food or taking rest no matter, you need to concentrate yourself that there is one target before your eyes.

I remember the day, while I was busy in firing, there was strong determination of one thing, 'target', I couldn't sense when the feeling of love spontaneously ridificated in heart and the dog of missing in the forest while we were both in acton group, in uniform and missing in forest. Nothing is remembered what was the date and time, we decided and promised looking at the fire of shifted cultivation, that we will start our family remaining ourselves in the party. Then the things of castration came to mind.

When I was preoccupied with the thoughts of castration, a letter with the messenger had come to be delivered. She had written in that letter in clear beautiful handwriting, "I want you, please come back to action. We need urgent to work in a single group adventurously, where and how operation starts, I will write - (Lal Salam) Red regards.

My heart filled hearten with this letter. I found myself energetic breaking my impassiveness. If I get her company after two days, then why should I delay for that work? I, on the spot, in presence of the same messenger, wrote a letter, "After fifteen days, you reach at the residence of Gunupur Engineer, Comrade, where the operation will be started."

That comrade friend of Gunupur, was staying in an empty lonely house with his wife and bedridden paralysed father. He, just working as an engineer in a private company nominally. He spends half of his salary for party's work. He was the disciple of Charu Majundar. Engineer sir, writes bulletin for party's vision and future action. His bearded face, careless costume a dirty bag reflect him a rough tuff man. The appearance suits him to carry a gun on shoulder instead of carrying the responsibility of family.

Once, I tapped on his door at ten O' clock night. We know him in code language - comrade Engineer. I conveyed 'Lal salam' he responded by the same regards. He looked around my hult here for twelve days". The unused garage room was cleaned and arranged a folding cot, a water pot, loongi-napkin, bedsheet, cloth, almost all required for a man, he arranged everything for me. I told him, there will be family planning operation, you arrange a doctor. We know, no govt. medical would be safe for me because police was in search for him, I stared at him.

The No. of days that I spent in that garage room the only waiting I had for that wheat colour, sparking eyes landlords. Whose love kept, me awaiting on the roped-cut for her arrival.

In one early morning, the engineer brought her to my room and left her there. She had taken a lot of strain for changing the vehicles in boarding from place to place, starting from Andra upto that place. After her arrival, it was decided for my operation in mid night.

We had only one day and a night in our hands. These two days were important time for us. Whether to achieve or to loss. Sometimes, we must have shed tears sometimes merrymaking laugh and pleasure.

My castration will achieve her, this brought of importency. I had to digest the manly counteract within me. But the thoughts and the pain of not becoming a mother of a child was swaying in her eyes. I picked her up onto my lap like a small child, and moved my palms cooly on her hair and consoled her. We should have love for our party first then marriage. Family we two with two members. We are energy for our party and vice versa. We are friends to walk on the blood bathing path. The party becomes strong by our loss and sacrifice. The revolution becomes firy. She understood and placed her hands with mine.

I felt severe pain after the power of anaesthesia decreased slowly after two days of operation. She stood up for parting and smiled and assured of meeting after three and half months. "Stay good comrade, take care of."

My future plan and dreams with the thoughts related to her preoccupied thought for me. At this moment, I received a message, that two greyhound of Andra in civil dress has kidnapped Dasu at railway station. No news about his absconding.

Dasu became a news. My condition became cool and calm after thunder strike. I became panic. We know the operation of Andra police on our party like holigans. If they have picked up Odisha man from Odisha, where are the police of Odisha.

I know the aggressiveness of Andra police, possibility is there, there may finish Dasu in encountering. They will stop the mouth of the Kuwi poet forever, who was the energy for Kuwi community, writing songs for them.

I have to go back to Raigada leaving behind the hospitality of the engineer, politics of Gunupur etc. I have to find out that dearest Kuwi poet Dasu. I left the dirty garage with the unsaved beard and moustache and dirty dress. I, remained in quest of the messenger, Niclash of Raigada. There was a hot discussion about kidnapping.

I received a bad news that police have made camps in short distances from the place, where I was. Prakash and Ravi, of Kadkamada village were arrested and interrogated in police station. They have been relieved. Police have started attacking on Dasuram village.

I asked, abou Gurudipanka. The condition of the Gurudipanka is certainly precarious, very bad sir, the Sundi, wine shopkeeper, the money lender those who were against the wine agitation of Dasu, they all have reaped riped corns from the field of Dasu. Police have already started loot in Gurudipanka village. Police have grabbed Rs. 1200/- and ration card from Paul Majhi, Cayenne, Chill, Kandul dal of Badisa Majhi, Kasu, Almond, ridge gourd of Kasu Malik, cooked beef of Makra Majhi and dried beef, kandul dal, ridge gourd from Sultan house. Police broke the lock of Prakash and entered into room but found nothing from his home. From the hand of ward member of Gurudipanka, police have snatched away six hundred rupees.

I just stopped him narrating the plunder of police in Gurudipanka, Niklas had returned from Gajapati district, and brought the news of oppression of police with him, he found very irritated. I put my hand on his head to cool down him by reminding him that police always apply the weapon, sharpen of both sides, we should not be disturbed at their one side operation, the party has trained us to be conscious of that.

Nicklas had come with an order for me that I have to leave the place Raigada immediately for Mohana. I have isolated myself from the Nicklas for set out my journey.

Though, months are passed, but neither the informer nor the messenger nor Missilia none of them could able to give any data about Dasuram. I was fear stricken, if they have killed Dasu on encounter. When I was wandering in the domain of dream in quite disturbed condition, a message was received that Dasu was in Viaskhapatnam jail.

I got back my sense. Dasu, O Dasu still alive. He was alive, my bad thoughts disappeared. He is saved from police encountered and presently in the prison of Visakhapatnam. What is he doing there? He must be sharpening his revolutionary song. In spite of busy schedule, I set out my journey out of happiness from Raigada district to Gajapati, from Gajapati to Berhampur, from Berhampur to Bhubaneswar. In the meantime, I have forgotten the art of counting the date of my marriage. She, to remind my forgetfulness, has written letter to me. A messenger had delivered that letter, after twenty days of this letter was written. She, in that letter, wrote, "Dear comrade! As per the norm and condition of party, a year has already been passed and along with it excess two months i.e., one year and two months. You let me know, when and where, we shall have meeting?"

After permission for marriage from the party, and in her fervency and aridity for marriage, I felt refloweringness of my love for her. Whereas, I was hurt by the absence of Dasu. In such auspicious and happiest moment of life, I could not accept his absence. I, immediately replied in a letter, in presence of the messenger to let he know, "We will marry, but our dearest comrade Dasu is not there to celebrate the occasion by singing an enchanting song - would you like to admit it a ceremony?" Dasu, has been transferred from Viaskhapatnam jail to G-Udaygiri jail of Odisha. You will receive my letter after his release from jail.

Delaying the date of marriage for Dasu's release was kept me discontent, but the news about Dasu, that was receiving from time to time were consoling me to keep in the state of happiness. I have got this news that the police was interrogating Dasu with corporal punishment and compelled him to admit as a Naxalite, but Dasu, in the third degree of punishment by police couldn't break his obstinacy and stubbornness. Dasu has been stood upright, wherever place it may be, may be under police custody or in the court. He has digested hard punishment for party.

For the programme of party, when I was present in Sapelguda village, there, the festival of Souras was going on. The dark night of Sapelguda was revealing and horse around by the song and dance of Soura's cultural programme. All were in drowsiness and sleeplessness next day. Mangera returned from Paralakhemundi.

Mangera was doing work for party. The eyes of the police were chasing after him in false case. He has been wandering in forest hiding, being escaped from jail twice. He told, "Sir, the news, I have with me, Dasu may be relieved after two people the bale has been arranged."

After detained for 16 months in jail, I left Sapelguda to meet that Kuwi poet, Dasu. I, in the residence of one of party supporter, I met Dasu there at Paralakhemundi. A man, got up from the surrounding of torture. Looked quite different. A shadow in the former shape. Still there were scars and wounds looked alive on his back. But the happiness of innocence of release from jail was glittering in his eyes.

Dasu paid me Lal Salam, with rummy eyes. I shook my hand with strong grip. I, on the beating wound of the back, touched them softly and sensitively. I asked, "when Andra police picked you up from station, was Odisha police present there.

I was urinating beside a hotel wall, near station. The Andra police in civil dress took me on the spot, no police of Raigada was there. I got down from the bike and retailed, "Why should I go with you sir? what's my fault, you take me to Odisha police and decide my crime." They beat me and made me sit in between forcefully. On the way they showed me another man who beckoned to take away, he was the man of our area. The informer of Andra police asked me for letter. I didn't have any letter with me, I just refused. They carried me to Kamrda police station and let me hold a bomd in my hand. "You're 'Naxalite, you declare yourself." I told, "I am not Naxlite. Why should I carry bomb in my hand?" They undressed me and put me in lock up."

I understood the emotion of Dasu, after returned from lock up how his expression was straight forward. "Tell me, there must be some persons relieved from police lock up of our party, you could have sent message in their hands about your detailed in lockup. We were baffled in your absence. We were in doubt whether you are alive or died in police encounter?"

"I laughed, saying the word 'finished', Dasu responded in smile. They did not keep me at any particular place constantly. How could I send message? They took me from Kamarda police station to Parvatipuram police station where, the police officer P. Vijaykumar beat me hard and snatched away my wristwatch and three hundred rupees. From that PS, both the police in joint platoon, took me to Vijaynagar. They interrogated me in a concealed room and put the gun's pipe into my mouth and asked, "Tell what do you know about Naxalite? Otherwise, you move with us Gudari wearing the Naxal dress. The police of Gunupur and Padmapur joined with them there. Odisha police beat me in such a way that the sticks were broken. Robber pipes were broken into pieces. An Odia old police told, "Let him sleep on rail line. There, they let me show slate written Jayaram Majhi, with the state, they took my photograph. Then they look me to Bobuli court, then to police station, then to the jail of Visakhapatnam. They accused me in false case and brought me back to Odisha through Vijaynagar and then to Paralakhemundi. Police have rolled me like kicked ball from station to station for sixteen months.

Dasu was glaring at the time of narrating this bitter experiences. The bone of Dasu was responding. I tried to make the situation light and asked, "Dasu! You must have composed a lot of songs inside jail?"

Dasu's appearance changed when I asked about song.

That song took me into jail. How would they give me chance of writing poems? There was neither pen nor paper. If I like to write anything, the only instrument was charcoal of the hearth. Though I couldn't write poem but prepared language alphabets for Kuwi people. He brought out a folded paper from his pocket and showed me scripts painted on it.

I gazed at Dasu's face in wonder. There was a thrilling of my voice. Are these Kuwi alphabets? Did you have these letters before?"

Dasu smiled and told, actually, there was no alphabet of our community. You better know, we write Kuwi language in Odia scripts. Once, I was asked by a policeman in G-Udaygiri police station - Ah! Poet do you write poems? People, the researchers team came to meet you. You became celebrity in everyday's newspaper. In which language, you write poems? Are they in Odia, Telegu or Hindi? I write in Odia language. "Why is there not any Kuwi script of your community?" the police asked me. I told no. if there is no script of your community. Then first you scrawl, show it to your people, let them learn, all will accept that aftermath. Since his suggestion, I have been scrawling these letters on the jail's floor. I completed it in six months duration of time.

Dasu let me introduce his scripts. Does he know what invention has made his Kuwi men? The community which has language but no scripts for writing, the existence of the language will disappear slowly. Dasu has succeeded inventing the scripts of his language. I wish to salute the first writer of Kuwi language what he deserved. I took the position and paid salute - Lal Salam - Red regards.

Dasu, with wonder and happiness stared at me. Do you know Dasu, Raghunath Murmu invented Adivasi language first and you the Kuwi scripts. Sir, I have no idea about invention what does it mean by. I wish to create scripts for our language. I have also thought, to publish a book for children with pictures for our people. They will learn this and write in our language.

Dasu seemed much satisfied with his work. When Dasu was in the world of dreamland. But I was happy because we would use these scripts as code language for some days. Police, if he come upon any letter written in this language will not understand anything either out of these alphabets or drawing. Dasu was found to be busy for his village, Gurudipanka. Neither his wife, none of them was allowed to meet him in jail. He was emotional to meet them without waiting.

How long could I break a man released from jail. Dasu set out his journey for home. Thereafter, for the party's work the time was fixed by busy scheduled programme. It was decided in upper level that there will be agitation and rally at Bhubaneswar. Therefore, there was contact with supporter of the party before that. We need to be vigilant on political situations there. I went on consulting people one after another and acted accordingly as per the direction of my commander.

In the busy schedule of the party and taking care of responsibility of the party, I came upon Paltu. A thing of greediness arose in me, when I came upon him. Anyhow, I will have to complete the marriage work within these work. Permission is most needful for performance this scared work. The co-ordinator of the party will have to fix the date and place of marriage and Paltu can take care of this with all sincerity.

I made him know, "You see you have to get arranged everything ready within fifteen days. Paltu, "rested me assure."

I remain in the world of dream till the permission from party is received. Then we will have mobile family live wandering from place to place. She was in my eyes in shalwar-punjabi and party's uniform, but on the marriage day, I will see her how she looks in saree? For the first time during the performance of sacred ceremony I will fold her arms on my chest of her shyness.

All my comrade friends and relatives will attend the party in one of the tribal village. They, the villagers will also derive pleasure out of this. Cows will be slaughtered, Mahuli wine will be in high emotion. Dasu will perform to his thrilling voice there. All will be dancing, singing. I will dance with her and slowly took her into forest under the canopy of moon and clouds, when all are in pick. The fragrance of the bunches of Kuwi flower. That is weared on the nut of her hair will spread the flavour through out forest.

I need a messenger of Andra area, who could diseminate my happiness to her. Paltu reached there, in the meantime. He let me receive the order of the zonal chief of Bansadhara. Dasu maleka needs to be present in press conference before the Janagarjan meet. The party has assured to fix up the date of my marriage after the convention.

Dream, automatically postpond to other days. I know, there is no value of a person the value of the party. Again, I encouraged for party. I began my journey to meet Dasu, Gurudipanka. I, now understand the importance of Dasu for party. In Bhubaneswar, convocation Dasu will stand amidst, reporter's, press media, tape recorder, camera Dasu will sing Kuwi song, composed by himself and show the Kuwi scripts that has experience as a prisoner for sixteen months. How Andra police are behaving on Naxalite, Dasu will expose that before mass media. Dasu will stands party of party's.

Once, the man who was composing songs for marriage and brides parting, his mission has become success. I reached at Gurudipanka and searched for him "Where is Dasu - Dasu."

Dasu amazed find me in his village. I told, "You will have to go to Bhubaneswar."

Dasu, after released from jail, could not find time to share times with his dear and nears.

He couldn't compose any song being punished severely by police could not sow any seed in his land. There may be jailed if he goes out. His mother denied out of fear. He can't go anywhere; a voice came inside of home.

I found, Dasu was sitting silently in the restriction of family members. There is no end of fighting. The fighter can't take rest at this time. I make myself more hard. I filled my voice with direction. His order of the party - you have to go.

Dasu with his Tambour, song pad, and a pika of sal leaves, left home for Bhubaneswar.

WHO MADE THIS MAN STONE?

Where the domain, the region of mountain, coils of streams and the forest of bamboo set their feet, They set their Basera the temporary tent there.

He feels hungry, free from all thoughts, finds the broken pieces of Jhikir stone under his feet. Sometimes he chew like a piece of biscuit in cracking sound. Got into the knee deep water of the half-dried Udanti-river. He bent down and drank palm full of water from her. Both his hunger and thirst was satisfied. Small eyes of him, look like the eyes of bats and small size belly like a crow. He eats in hungry whatever he finds. Bamboo's malt. Kuner green. Sweet potato fat rice. It is better to chew small pieces of Jhikir stone to meet hunger than eating fat rices. There is much satisfaction in it.

Hunger can't scare of him. He stands straight back to hunger like bamboo tree looking at the footpath of the forest route. He usually sits in one place but in mind he wanders up and down in search of bamboo trees in dense forest. The bamboo bush hidden in the abyss of toe heaps of hills and the leaves are reflected in sunshine, he reached there. The commotion of wild birds and the sound of flutter, songs of cricket as if they are talking with the dumbed forest. He has to do a hard labour to reach at the spot through dingle and jolty paths. He looks greedly the bamboo stand upward looking into the sky. He thinks about the fat bamboo whether to cut or wait for young trees to grow fat, he wanders in the world of dream, thinks about the future seriously. But eardrops the presence of bears. The fear of the command of the forest guard is very fearful than the walking sound of the bear, very heedful. At the same time he heard rattling of the rats in his stomach. The attempt with axe instruct him, "Cut and pull out from the deep bush, he got sweated. He cut the kani-branches from bamboo, split it into wicker and made bundle to carry them home. In home, again he split that spars into thin wicks and dried them up in sunshine to make basket. Creel, bhoga, topa, winnowing fan like an artist. The business man buys all the bamboo products from him and bring then to market and villages for selling. The money he got in exchange of bamboo products make his mind idle for someday. He never thinks of going to forest for collection of bamboo until the money is spent completely. His hunger increases when the money is spent. Then his hands move automatically in search of jhikir stone to meet his need of food.

That day, he threw that bundle of bamboo in yard and ran to field for excrete. He looned deep like coal goose in the water of Udanti river to make cool his sweated body. He sploshed his belly in waist deep water and got up. It was of intensive hot of midday, no one was seen anywhere. He made himself naked and sueezed the wet napkin and wiped his wet body with that and ashored. He paid respect to the stone idol of Nangal Debata installed under that sal tree. He heard someone called him from the nearby field - 'Aey come here.'

The owner of the land was standing with an umbrella in the excrete field, Gupadia. His residence was across the river. The years together uncultivated barren land was filled with crape by the village people. Sometimes he comes to look after the land and returned grumbled and displeased with the inhabitants.

'This is your excrete?' the owner using the napkin mask asked him standing in front of the fresh crape.

'Hay'. Why should he fear of him? I have been excreting in this field since long. All the villagers of Langalghat have been using the land long days before. Is it new today?

Does my excrete look white-'dhab nei disbar'? Why does it look white? Tell me! What have you eaten? "Kan tui Khaesu?"

When I feel hungry. I eat Jhikir stone. What then 'Ar kana'?

The land owner understood everything from this. 'Okay', He warned, "Don't excrete in my land from today. If it is, I will put you in the police station."

No, no sir. I beg pardon, bent down on his feet. The land owner went on searching for white excrete from corner to corner of the land and left with grumbling. Someday passed.

He was cutting wicken with knife to make them thinner and thinner by stretching his legs from the yard. The works to shift the crops from field was very close. The business men will come to village to buy, basket bhoga, topa, winnowing far, all bamboo products. He will earn some money. He gives all that earnings to the piyusi Anti hand. His piyusi aunt was dangling me in a cradle with a sari fled like a baby elephant from one eaves to other eaves in the low height thatched roof. Daughter of my Aunt, Dhanamati, fly like silk cotton from door to door of the village. Dhanamati is lame for a polio from her childhood. But her eyes were flashing like bobbing water waves of the Uddanti river chhalmal. She blossomed from sixteen to seventeen. Her Polio-lameness, and short height distract all dhangdas for Dhanamati of Langalghati village. My Aunt always thinks to express her emotion but stopped and kept herself mum. Sometimes she remembers and recollects all about her past time sitting under the eaves.

He could not estimate the time, where he started and where he reached? And where to reach? He fumbled and feels nerd when the thought of his own strikes to his mind. How could he forget the fragrance of and attachment of Khudupali village? That Khudapali is surrounded by forest and mountains. There are pith, honey, banji mushroom, bamboo karadi, bunjhei green leave and meat of the wild animals. His small but smiles with the wolf of his maiji woman. The infant in the womb of Hemabati was now towing the tiny fish. Her feet were swelling and walking was very slow as well as way of talking. Her slowness of everything sacrificed the suffering from birthday pain. There was a lot of hue and cry among the women of Khudupali a child will born of Mangul Majhi. Her birth pain has already started.

All the women in support of their hands and shoulders had carried Hemabati and pulled her inside to the lonely villa, a rough and small height thatched hut. That is the only delivery house / birth place 'Antari ghara' of Khudupalli village. Night in the windowless delivery house had painted her darkness like mud on the walls of Antari hut. Straws was littered on the ground and a date leaves mat spread over it. An earthen pot filled with water was kept in the corner of the room. Some tattered clothes were fallen beside her. It was the only Antari delivery house of the village. All but he himself were born in this room. His body will born in that house. The nurse along with Maiji and other women bolted the door inside. Others remain busy in chatting, sitting on the yard. He sat leaning against the maula tree. Hemabati was fighting alone for birth of the body. The air, outside the delivery house was vibrating at the sound of cry and pain. "Bua go' 'Maa go'. All, outside the room were eaves dropping the cry of baby and the shouting of the Nurse, 'Pilahari'. The door of Antighar will open after that. Then all the waiter of outside will enter into the room. Some of them will go for fire the hearth to boil the water, someone will cut the navel's cord. If a daughter is born, her navel cord will be cut with the top of arrow head iron. The baby will be washed. Baby will suck milk from mother's breasts. Both mother and baby will return home. The Antari room will remain closed till the birth of a maiji of anyone of the village.

The pain of sobbing 'Kohanala' was heard to outside. The sunshine was flowing to midday from the softness of the morning sunshine. All the women of the village waiting for the sound of cry of the baby, were dozing there. He could predict everything sitting beneath the tree. His maiji due to failure of delivery and birth pain was rolling on the ground crying with pain like python. A baby, as all dream will certainly come out, they all also, were praying for this. His navel cord will be cut. He had tiled two things in his napkin and kept them carefully. He, to make the device sharper in hone for smooth cutting had made them updated and scrubbed. A pots herd and an arrow head, sharped pick. Be it a male or female, whatever baby may it be. One of them will be applied and worked out. He will be fathering to that baby. The curve of his family number will go up.

Midday was descending down. The cracked sounds like potsherd of earthen pot was coming out from that Antari ghara and emerged in air. Her voice was chocked for shouting and crying and lost all her strength and energy and got silence - My Hemabati. Still the cry of a baby. Kuan Kuan was heard to outside. When she had tried to open the door and run away but protected by the women of Khudupani village, maiji the oldest women.

Wait… wait. The mother-sarth, as she has given birth us, likewise we suppose to surrender a child on her lap before enter into the Antari Ghara delivery room. Neither sun or the moon, none of them could see out birth. This tradition has been prevailing since three generations in our pariha community. Still he asked with emotion and absecration, "Tar radakirla or ta suni hebar" - why her shouting and screaming is not heard further?" not heard the cry of that newly born baby - "janam pilar kanda kata bita nahin sunibar."

There was no sound from that delivery room - Antarighar since long. The sun shine was withering in the wings of the nest-returning birds. Day is not ready to leave the earth so far but the delivery hut was encircled by gloominess. A bhusan, the woman shouted, the moment she had entered into the room, "She is no more - "she an jiban dharikari naina."

Who is no more? Baby or her mother? Mother or her baby? All these questions shucked his heart like electric current. He trotted and ran rushing into that delivery room madly. Hemabati was laying cold flat like a piece of stone slab. A baby had just shown his head in birth canal - Billa. Fresh nub-fleshly blood adequate, foam was flooded around her, they all turned stone like hard things.

He dragged himself steps back from Antari ghara. Backed to his own home. Left Khudupani village back. Daring to darkness of night, wild animals, bumpy footpath, hills, he went on walking. He felt, as if he did not have legs, but flew like a piece of straw. Night was over. He reached at Langalhat village. Knocked at the door of piusi-aunt Didi Didi O.

He could fly away, if any one had touched his body. This was the condition of him. Both mother and daughter took him into home and gave him water and let him speak his problems before them. He felt energetic. Didi told, "you are the son of my brother, you may not have any problem." You may stay and earn your livelihood here. You are my another child come here.

If she would have another child. He had tried the best to forget all about the past, he squeezed him completely. He has not forgotten to search the bamboo bushes in jungle in spite of his frustration. He cuts bamboo and makes baskets, bhoga etc. He split in two pieces hive bamboo. One day Didi told him, "You take the responsibility of Dhanamali, she is lame. You both stay here. Both take care of each other, "You build your future."

Another family means another Antari ghara, delivery house. Another premature death. All the inauspicious thoughts made him husband fool. Dhanamati stood at threshold eaves drop. Dhanamati turned her face to a bundle of cloth-bag hanged on wall and put her face out of shame. Someone from village came and called him, "Come here". Two outsiders have come, they asked for you-dui baharia luka tote khujanarie ashichan.

He boggled and spooked. What works were there of the outsiders with him. They were waiting for him in front of sate Langal idols. They were owner of the land the known one and other one was attired in cap, goggles, camera, quite unknown man to him. The owner of land took him to the patch of land. That young man was telling, will you excrete today? Ali Athan Hagibuta? He was trying to ask something but the landowner showed him - 'behold'. He is not alone, other five or six persons have been excreting. All that stools look white colour. Nothing striked to his mind. But he felt relaxed because he was not the only man doing that but others were there. Stool of his own not only look white colour but others too. Almost all the stool of many of Langalghat looks white. The photographer had taken the snaps of all that heap of stools and asked him, "Do you eat jhikiri stone? He does not hesitate to tell the truth about his food stuff. Its shame for those who do not eat. Its common and day to day matter for him. He smiled nodding his head and reciting - 'hal' - 'hal' - well! Which variety of stone you eat? Let me see how you eat them? The photographer became enthusiastic to see this with action.

They all entered into the village. People of twenty five houses stood around him. The land owner addressed all of them one after another and told, "This is a reporter", He will collect information 'Jankavi' about you and propagate you on TV. "Govt's Jhumura phankaba." All your plight will be ended. Gariba Hatiba-poverty will be eradicated." They did not know what is poor. How could they know the reporter and his works? They had set up their habitations in the forest land. They live on fruits and flowers of forest and make bamboo products for creating funding. They manage their bread and butter by any means. But they didn't have any experiences of poverty. They didn't have any idea about comparing one man with another man. Whereas the landowner and the reporter, they were uttering poor and poor.

The reporter enquired to know why these people are poor after achievement of independence since long days.

Sir, How couldn't they remain poor? They are the most ancient tribal inhabitants of Nuapada. They are

Praharia. They supposed to be included among the lists of ancient tribal inhabitants. But in the list of Tribal community the officer had mentioned them as potter. Sir! Listen me, the people who do the job of irons. Weapons are called OBC. But those Praharis know nothing about blacksmith. The officer didn't understand the different between iron work and bamboo works. They have been enlisted as blacksmith, OBC in place Praharia, the most ancient Tribal community in the list of Govt. Govt's. funding comes for ST and SC but not for OBC. So, unfortunately they remain neglected for ever.

The land owner was man of this locality. He knew all about the miserable conditions of the Praharia community. He had brought the reporters to Langalghat village to do something for these down trodden under developed people. The reporter wanted to know if there was any attempt had been made to make them Tribal? "Who will plead on behalf of them? Their number is about four thousands, the people who suffox to do. Perhaps the politicians would have done this if their number had more than four to five lakhs. You may investigate, that the praharis of Chhattisgarh, adjacent to their habitants are enjoying the privilege of praharia, as the tribal men in the list of Chhattisgarh Govt. whereas these ancient Tribal community praharia of Nuapada, Kalahandi, Bolangir, Bargad are in the list of OBC. Nobody has made any effort to include and enlisted them in the list of tribal.

They didn't have idea about themselves. They could understand that both were talking about their welfare. The complicated language and conversation in between them had made the mind stone of all the people of Langalghat. The only thing they could understand that they were poor.

The camera boy was busy for preparing a story for TV news. The land owner appears to be happy as he did a great job for parihas. Both of them entered into knee deep water of Udanti river and went across her. All the people of Langalghat were gazed and gazed at them. Riding the white vehicle, the reporters and the owner, they were lost in the narrow path of the dense forest.

Evening passed. The darkness of night vanished and dipped the white stools, poverty and Govt. of Langalghat. All the thought of the villagers was lost in their dreams.

Sometimes, like previous incident, some outsiders visit to Langalghat village to collect information about plights of the villagers. Some of them take snaps and some of them nictitate for Mahuli wine. Some of them dance out of intoxication. They ask for dance and song and they assure to pay money in exchange. They ask many questions. They say, there will be research on your community. That will be published in newspaper. There will not be any problem of yours. All the outsiders think many things about Parihas on many ways with different intention. He termed them padara insects, the insects.

A butterfly for pirching was flying on his face in dream. He rose his hands to drive out it. His sleep was broken by clanging of something else. His did was calling him by clanging the bamboo baskets lent against the wall. It was almost first or second half of the night. She entered into the room by opening the wattling. Dhanamati was standing in the dim light of Lantham and half opened door.

Didi found her standing, she started to talk. Listen! Manglu, how long would you sleep on yard. I know, you keep warm your pocket by selling bamboo products. He had kept his ears open to listening her talk in half sleep state like tode. Didi went on saying "You must be observing that Dhanmati is growing old. What is difference between uncle's son and jue or son-in-law. If you don't understand you who would like to convince you? Are you listening my words or not?"

Haie! Yes! Anunty. He curled himself like a dog in sleep and remained silence but Didi went on talking chasing after him in talk. Your uncle has acquired a patch of land in langalghat village. You may build a hut there. And make Dhanmati your maieji-wife and proceed with a happy marital life.

Now I'm two twenty and five. 'Dui kodi panch helan'. Dhanmati is at sixteen-seventeen- 'sul satarar Tukkle aei.'

Why do you sit silently? "Basti kan a achhare baboo?" Have you seen the marriage of pariah people? "Amar parihas bibha hebake ken bais deksi kain-ei ganre sansarkar raha." You live a marital life here and live with pleasure.

This advice of aunt enmeshed his thoughts, as he lost in one marital life past. He was bathing in sweating being excited out of these halk of his Aunt. But Didi eaves dropped to his respond. She was looking with her glowing eyes like glow worm beside the half opened wattling. Dhanmati avoided that thing and told let me think over the matter later. "Dekhmi chintakari kahemi goo!"

Towards ending part of the night, he had got little sleep, along with that, the face of Dhanmati and the expression of her innocent eyes Dhanmati was waiting opposite side of the door. She turned up and put out the lantharn. He also listened the cry of bears, the flapping sound of wings of Bats, hooting of owls, and croaking of frogs throw out nights. In dream, he was watching the limping of Dhanamati. Her head/ brain was occupied with a thought of family. She was mending the roof. That dreams were wandering like a gipsy but time was up and it became morning.

Returning from forest in midday sunshine carrying

the bundle of bamboo wickers on head, he came to know that the camera man and some other important persons have arrived their village. They were enquiring about Mangul pariah. All the strain and pain of bamboo wicker was disappeared. He stood upright being countered among important people of the village. Listen everybody! The photographer boy told all about your village Langalghat was played on TV. Whole assembly was fussed by hue and cry. The opposition people demanded for an investigation. There will be an investigatory committee. You all will be included in about the thing that you eat as food. Would you like to speak the truth?

They didn't have an idea about assembly. They don't know who were opposite members? Even they didn't have knowledge how to investigate. For which they were listening everything silently. Many thoughts jumbled their minds. A camera boy from the crowd had tried to match the eyes with theirs and taught like a teacher. Do you eat jhikir stone out of hunger sometimes? We know parihas never speak lie. Confess if it is fact or fiction?

They nodded their heads being heard the credits of Parihas. If any sahibs come to enquire the matter, you should speak to them truth. If you reveal the truth then your misery may disappear.

They are poor, they expressed the truth emotionally. Nobody, even a single outsider had turned up for a long days. For parihas morning shows the light with red tea, fried flour and make basket, dalla, bhoga, topa, kula and tala etc. from bamboo wicks. They mill rice with a pestle collect pitch, Banji mushrooms in jungle. Though the entire village was dipped with their thoughts of works, the things of marriage and the emotions about it was cohered in the neck of Dhanamati. Its only her mother could grasp the inner feelings of her daughter. Once she had showed a fench surrounded patch of land of Mangal by holding his hand.

Yes! Come. This is your place. Collect Khamna-pillars, wood, bamboo for building of the house.

He pretended if he has heard nothing of Didi's advice. I don't have money with me. "Moor thane ihande paisa naina." Let some days pass.

Okay. Try to get it done in leisure time - subidha dekhi maite, Bail pakei ghar dihike majbut kar. Then you think of making home.

Yes! My dear Didi.

He rest his Didi assured and released the burden of fear.

Next day, the outsiders crowded the village Langalghat again. Everyone was addressing to each other by the position of sarapanch, Badababu and BDO and so on. The right hands or the stunch supporters of the leaders, or the power holders were addressed in their supporters of the leader, or the powerholders were addressed in their ways. Perhaps two or may be three, they had never seen the Sarapanch earlier. They were mere listeners. Sarapanch address them as people of Govt. They have come to your village before the visit of investigatory committee. They want to know about your problems. They want to know whether you eat jhikir stone out of hunger or not? If this is true they may get arranged everything to remove all your problems.

BDO sir with an inquisitiveness enquired to know, "Is it fact that you eat stone?" all were silent. Mangal was there. He exposed the reality. "Yes Sir! We have eaten sometimes - 'Kebe kenta ame khalisu.'

'Stop' - A shout, as if a gust of wind dropped the dry leaves of trees of forest.

From today, right now, you the Paharias don't utter

that you eat stones. Remember very well with a voice of threatening.

A man, from the crowd, in white clad came front who glared with the hard voice like a mad elephant squeled the crops. They could not understand their fearful intention hidden behind their white clads and gentle appearance. But, the oldest man of the village tried to make them understand, "Our ancestors had been eating this, so as we. This is the reality sir."

A man, perhaps the right hand lieutenant of sarapanch shouted with warning, "We don't know what is truth or lie?" the Badababu, head babu of Samajhdar Behera who tried to pacify the thing and told in soothing voice." Whatever things are being told by babu, everything is for your wellbeing, when you cut bamboo to make wicks for baskets talla or dalla, are you not splintering them? If one portion is true. Other one is false. Are you not using the splinted bamboo in work or not? Now, try to understand what is truth, the same is false, no difference. One of them reminded the BDO sir, listen! Its only fifteen days time with us for the arrival of the committee members. Let us built the house of Anganwadi, then repairing of the buildings of the villagers. New building will be constructed. Morums, red colour soil will be spread on the road. Lot of things are to be prepared.

Yes sir, everything will be done in time sir. If its started tomorrow all expected works will be completed within seven days. The contractor assured the BDO sir repeatedly.

BDO sir rested the villagers assured, "Right now you won't have any problems. Hunger can't compel you to eat stone, no more, not at all, rest assured."

The soothing sayer BDO's voice made everyone

sweet. Thereafter, head clerk, other officers went on inquiring the conditions of the people from door to door. They prepared a list about the condition of the houses. Followed these activities, the sarapanch was giving assurance with smiling face putting hands on shoulders of people. The maeji, dhangra and dhangries had paid their attention with open ears enthusiastically. The aunt of Mangal came out holding his hands. She introduced to sarapanch sir, "This is my nephew. He has nothing identity here. This is his patch of land. You please make for him a building.

Sarapanch passed this news to BDO sir. BDO instructed the clerk to prepare a list. The sun didn't pay any regards to the list of BDO, clerk and other officials rather wheeled towards western horizon. They all remain busy in coming and going, doing works. A clever man, like the cunningness of a jack, put a beetle in mouth and started chewing that and spoke giving assurance that all problems will be over right from tomorrow. You may see off us today. A reputed committee will visit after this accompanied by renowned doctors. If you tell, that you eat stone out of hunger, they will cut your belly with knife to have a test of it.

Some of us were quite scared of operation. They tried not to indulge in any complexities of operation of belly wonder. The nights hear solved in morning's sun shine. A group of pumbler arrived with equipments to bore a tubewell. They solved water problem in two days. The women of Langalghat forgot the Udanti river and stood in a queue with coloured buckets, water pots in front of the tube well for water. Village looked smiling. The tractor loaded by red moharum came rushing entered into Langalghat village. Red hard soil was spread all over the footpath from the idol of Langal god to end of the village.

The abyss and crevasse road were filled by red hard soil. The village looked red. Red soil coloured the village street. A truck-lorry came loaded by wood and items for construction of Anganwadi. House. Such as wooden pillar, bamboo, tiles. Half constructed buildings were repaired. The houses of homeless people were constructed within two days.

Once Didi reminded him, when she was serving food in midday, your house has been made. You may decide about Dhanamati now don't forget.

He picked up green chilly along with fried green leaves and made sound out of irritation of it and drank rice water up to brim and hiccuped with sour. He spoke, don't dream on outsider's assurance. Didi

Listen! Everything will be set right, as the Govt. has come to our place. He didn't respond but continued his eating silently. The coman's vehicles come to Langalghat one after another only because of him. He smiled by himself.

Outsiders, just after two days, arrived with bag and baggages at Langalghat village and gave away rice packets of fifty kgs weight, dal, oil, lantern, pocket of kirana in every house. They distributed sari for women, imitation necklace, ear rings, bangles and many fashionable items for women. You the paharias enjoy your lives like queen with the things.

He found his Didi and Dhanamali were plaster basket full of soil here, Didi told.

Looking at the busy schedule of progress Mangal thinks all these developments are not less than the work of a magician. Rice and grocery items were nearby their hand. Roof, overhead. He will stay here with his maiji Dhanamati. Again, Mahul flower will blossom in his life.

Anganwadi Madam accompanied by a helper reached in the village along with so many things. Kirana, cooking items, play items, egg, picture books, shirt pant and many. Anganwadi Didi moved from door to door with friendly attitude. They made friendship with every and each woman of Langalghat. A list of four to six years children were prepared. Children will be provided with new shirt and pants.

They told that helper Didi would come tomorrow to take children to school. There school uniforms will be given away. They will read there. Midday meal will be given to them, then children will come back home. You please send them to school. They will be made good human being. All will be well.

Parents become emotional when they are assured about the betterment of their children. Next day, like cattle, Anganwadi helper came and collected all children to school. They were put on new dress and shoes and washed their hands with soap. Then fried flatten rice and sweet ball were given away in breakfast. Didi taught them songs, dance, stories as well as provided crayon colour box, drawing copy etc. children were taught playing. Then children ate delicious dishes rice, eggs curry. Now Anganwadi Didi carried them to their home.

All the children of our village glew like morning sun shine and village grew with pleasure happiness. This time my aunt Didi tied Dhanamati with me in cupidal knot. With some cocks and the freely provided rations my aunt had arranged a feast on the occasion of marriage. The freely provided ornaments, necklace, bangles, ear rings were being put on by Dhanamati and looked like fresh corn flower maeji and fluttering wings. Happiness of the home-returned children was bobbling in the eyes of children like dream. As if these children were floating like paniculate rain clouds over the vales and hills of the dense forest. They were knowing so many things. And eat palatable dishes. Actually, I need children with these attitudes. He will certainly go to Anganwadi. He will be paniculate clouds in their company. Observing all these he was flying by mounting the Pegasus.

Like unseasoned rain clouds the outsiders entered into village groupwise. They brought and supplied kerosene, rice in every door. They gathered Dokra Dokri, Dhangda Dhangdi, Maeijies women in the village. They instructed and threatened that the higher authority is coming to your village tomorrow. If they ask about your problem, then tell them we have everything stock and sumptuous, nothing is deficit. If you answer them in other language negatively, you will suffer. To greet the sir, you all put on new saree and ornaments provided to you and welcome them into village with singing and dancing.

Truly, next day, a high officer, accompanied by the Collector, BDO, Forest Officer, Police Officer, all reached in a Kaman vehicle. Every and each mam pf Langalghat appears like a unopened file. The officers manoeuvre with every and each file. They asked to all Anganwadi children about their wellbeing. "Are you eat meal there? Do you love to go there? The officer asked. "Yes!" They nodded their heads.

One officer asked to a Dokri, "Do you have food stuff in your home or not? Are you not stay hungry?" the Dokri had pointed her showing towards toppled rice packets. "Well! do you have enough food to eat or you stay hungry?" Another officer asked. Again he asked, "Do you eat stone?"

He had a fear for operation of belly what he heard from a man. They claimed to tell the officers three things. He uttered like a trained parrot, "We have rice, we are not hungry, we are perfectly well."

He was standing keeping tobacco leaves dust in mouth since long. He threw that with spite out.

All the investigations and inquiries were over with satisfaction. The officers were tired moving from door to door. A man was roaming like a rat, said with great sighy everything was completed okay. "Thanks to Praharia."

They were little aware of the meaning, well done, Sabas. They knew the two splited bamboo, one is right, other one is wrong i.e. sabas. They were quite ignorant about the percentage of water and components available in that. But everything changed in blinking of eye.

After departure of the committee, neither the food stuffs, commodities nor Anganwadi Didi, non of them was there. They had returned to the place, where they had come from. The Anganwadi centre looked deserted. That ten days life style : new dress, palatable foods, storytelling, singing dancing programme had made their children saheb and they had to return to their own position to that muddy games.

One day the contractor reached with lorry and loaded it with all the furniture and broke that Anganwadi centre to take everything with him.

Some of us requested them not to break the structure and to let that structure remain stand as the symbol of progress of Langalghat village.

The contractor made them understand that all the things were brought in rent and they would be returned to the owner.

The tube well, the only one remain stood barren still there like a mile stone. Again, weeds grew at the place of Anganwadi. There was nothing remain at the memory of the incidents. The outsiders such as suppliers, grocery suppliers and others were not seen in other helps, they all became beggars again. They had revived their skills of cutting bamboos and going into forest in search of food. They required money to buy salt, oil and other food items. Again time brought back the past deserted days to Langalhat. Again hunger made them run into forest. Again they all bent down in making basket, Tala, bhoga, topa from bamboo wickers.

No outsiders remain preserved in mind except the people, women, Dhangra, Dhangri, Dokara, Dokri of Langalghat village. His was growing with the age. The power of his eyes and stamina of hands were detoriating. Dhanmati was very young dhangri, maiji-wife, a long route lies before her to do hard work for her bread and butter.

In afternoon he was in off mood. Many thoughts had overcrowded his mind. He came to night soil. The field was filling with white stools than the yellow coloured stool of Govt. provided freed cost rice.

Come here, Dhanamati was calling angrily. Dhanmati has a quality to recognise her men looking at the stools. He left the night soil and reached at Dhanamati.

Semi darkness had spread its sheet from forest to Langalghat village and dipped it. Dhanamati came close to him. He held the hand of Dhanamati and led her towards the idol of forest God. Dhanmati could not understand his purpose. He was stepping ahead with his own thoughts. As if small children were running from schools after eating sumptuous meals happily. Singing songs whatever they liked, this scene was dancing before his eyes and again they disappear in darkness. He could listen high recitation of Anganwadi Didi and low soft voice of helper Didi. All that sounds disappeared in air. He will have his own child. He will go to Anganwadi. All his dreams for future as if lost at that place in fog.

The trees stood like black ghosts and were making sweeping sounds. There was not a single tree in this field for the shelter of ghosts. They had cut down all the trees to build a house, they took away all that wood logs by ex-

interested that was receding in earth. It was only the high mounted hearth in rain and sunshine. Dhanmati sat beside that hearth out of exhaustion. All of sudden, she thought there must be heat of the hearth, she touched that ashes. He took the cold palm of Dhanamati into the palm to warm up her palm. Perhaps she felt warm in his clutch and reclined on his chest. He had vanity upon the entire world eyes became wet out of sobbing.

He asked him, "You're poor, what do you know?"

Laugh bursted his mouth. He told to Dhanmati like an experienced man, "I don't understand anything about poor or rich. The rich men came and made all the paharias rich then made us poor again.

He groped two jhikir stone in darkness and gave away one piece to Dhanamati and took one to his mouth. There was no sound except the grawing and grating sound of stones. Darkness turned into stone slowly.

BLACK EAGLE BOOKS

www.blackeaglebooks.org
info@blackeaglebooks.org

Black Eagle Books, an independent publisher, was founded as a nonprofit organization in April, 2019. It is our mission to connect and engage the Indian diaspora and the world at large with the best of works of world literature published on a collaborative platform, with special emphasis on foregrounding Contemporary Classics and New Writing.

www.ingramcontent.com/pod-product-compliance
Lightning Source LLC
Chambersburg PA
CBHW020152120726
47903CB00007B/2514